PUFFIN BOOKS

Dragon Boy

Dick King-Smith was born near Bristol. After serving in the Grenadier Guards during the Second World War, he spent twenty years as a farmer in Gloucestershire, an experience which inspired many of his stories. He went on to teach at a village primary school. His first book, *The Fox Busters*, was published in 1978. Since then he has written a great number of children's books including *The Sheep-Pig* (winner of the *Guardian* Award), *Harry's Mad*, *Noah's Brother*, *The Hodgeheg*, *Martin's Mice*, *Ace*, *The Cuckoo Child* and many others. He is married with three children and ten grandchildren, and lives in Avon.

Dragon Boy

Dick King-Smith

Illustrated by
Jocelyn Wild

PUFFIN BOOKS

PUFFIN BOOKS

Published by the Penguin Group
Penguin Books Ltd, 27 Wrights Lane, London W8 5TZ, England
Penguin Books USA Inc., 375 Hudson Street, New York, New York 10014, USA
Penguin Books Australia Ltd, Ringwood, Victoria, Australia
Penguin Books Canada Ltd, 10 Alcorn Avenue, Toronto, Ontario, Canada M4V 3B2
Penguin Books (NZ) Ltd, 182–190 Wairau Road, Auckland 10, New Zealand

Penguin Books Ltd, Registered Offices: Harmondsworth, Middlesex, England

First published by Viking 1993
Published in Puffin Books 1994
1 3 5 7 9 10 8 6 4 2

Text copyright © Fox Busters Limited, 1993
Illustrations copyright © Jocelyn Wild, 1993
All rights reserved

The moral right of the author has been asserted

Filmset in 13/16 pt Monophoto Baskerville
Printed in England by Clays Ltd, St Ives plc

Contents

I

'Not Even a Little One'

The dragon opened his huge mouth, with its rows of long sharp teeth, and belched.

It was not only a very loud belch, it was also visible, for it emerged in the shape of a blue flame.

'Montagu Bunsen-Burner!' cried his wife. 'Where are your manners?'

'I do beg your pardon, my dear,' replied her husband. 'It was that last knight I ate last night. Tinned food never agrees with me, it is so hard to digest.'

'Then I shall have to put you on a diet,' said Mrs Bunsen-Burner. 'Nothing but sheep or swine or oxen from now on. That should be no great hardship – a bullock of goodly size is better for you than a knight, any day.'

'I know,' said Montagu. 'It's not that I really like the taste of the fellows – so metallic, you know, sets my teeth on edge. It's just that they are such a confounded nuisance, forever challenging every dragon they meet, with their great long lances and their silly swords. One simply has to eat them to get a bit of peace and quiet. Yesterday's one was typical. I was having a snooze in the forest, minding my own business, harming neither man nor beast, when this damned fellow comes galloping up, shouting, "Have at thee, Fiendish Worm! Thy end is nigh!" and stuff like that. Then he points his lance at me and cries, "Prepare to die!" Same to you with knobs on, I thought, and I swallowed him down and had the horse for afters.'

Montagu belched again but more discreetly, placing one scaly paw over his mouth.

'I'll warrant you did not cook the horse properly,' said Mrs Bunsen-Burner. 'You know how delicate your stomach is. I'm not saying you can do much about a knight in full armour – you have to have them cold – but something the size of a charger ought to be properly barbecued. You have only yourself to blame.'

'Yes, dear,' said Montagu.

'Right then,' said Mrs Bunsen-Burner. 'No more knights until I say so. Is that understood?'

'Yes, dear,' said Montagu meekly.

During many years of wedlock he had learned, sometimes painfully, that it was best to give way to his wife, and it was seldom that he summoned up the courage to oppose her will, which was of iron. There was not a dragon in the length and breadth of Merrie England, he told himself, that would dare stand up to Albertina Bunsen-Burner.

There were ways of getting round her, however, and one, which Montagu found especially effective, was flattery.

To understand his use of it, you must realize that dragons' comments upon each other's appearance are the exact opposite of what we humans say. 'Beautiful', 'handsome', 'pretty', 'good-looking' – these are all words that any self-respecting dragon hopes never to be called, for they indicate the scorn, contempt or downright loathing of the speaker.

Ugliness of form and feature is what every dragon takes pride in, and a standard compliment would be one such as Montagu now paid Albertina. To give it added weight, he used his pet name for her.

'Hotlips,' he said in a sugary voice.

The look in Albertina's blood-red eyes softened.

'Yes, Monty?' she said.

'Oh, Hotlips!' said Montagu. 'You are by far the most hideous dragon in the land!'

Albertina positively bridled. She would have fluttered her eyelashes if she had had any.

'Oh, Monty!' she said. 'You say the nicest things.'

'Yes,' said Montagu. 'I know. Now, about this diet . . .'

'No knights!' said his wife, changing her tone sharply. 'We shall never solve your digestive problems if you continue to consume large quantities of metal. That is the reason for your attacks of flatulence. I thought I had made myself clear on this point, Montagu?'

'Oh yes, dear, yes, you have. Certainly no knights, but I was wondering . . . what about lesser humans – yeomen, freemen, goodmen, woodmen, serfs, the odd varlet, that sort of thing? None of those are armour-bearing, and, despite the fact that the creatures are so awfully beautiful, I am rather partial to human flesh, lightly roasted. The little ones are particularly tasty – not unlike sucking-pig. Surely I might be allowed an occasional human, Hotlips my love?'

Mrs Bunsen-Burner considered this request. She regarded her huge husband and thought how perfectly revolting he looked. He's a foul figure of a dragon, she said to herself with pride, but nonetheless he's weak-willed. If I allow him a swine-herd or two, he'll be back on the knights before you know it.

'No, Montagu,' she said firmly. 'Humans are off the menu. Anyway, I don't believe they are good for you, armour or no armour. They're too stringy and bony and generally indigestible – bound to be constipating. No, you stick to livestock. No people.'

'Not even a little one?' said Montagu.

'Not even a little one.'

Which made things hard for Montagu Bunsen-Burner, that very afternoon.

Last night's knight at last digested, he spread his leathery wings and flew away above the great green sea of trees, peering down into the glades on the lookout for deer or wild boar or forest ponies.

For a while he had no luck, for any animal that came into view bounded, trotted or galloped away into the safe cover of the greenwood before Montagu could set himself for a dive.

Then suddenly, as he swooped low over a clearing, he heard a wailing noise, and banking and turning, saw beneath him the figure of a small boy.

Fists pressed against his streaming eyes, the child sat with his back to an oak tree, crying his heart out.

I could soon stop that racket, thought Montagu. It's only a mouthful. And she'd never know. But then it occurred to him that his wife might smell barbecued boy on his breath, so he changed his mind.

Strangely though, the wailing began to affect him in some way. I must be getting soft, said Montagu Bunsen-Burner to himself, and he planed down and landed.

'Now, now, sonny,' he said in as gentle a voice as he could manage. 'What's the trouble?'

At these words the small boy took his fists from his eyes and stared up at the great dragon before him. His clothes were ragged and his feet bare. Poor little chap, thought Montagu. Pity he's so pretty, but that's not his fault. At least he's stopped that awful yelling.

'Don't worry,' he said. 'My wife's put me on a diet. No humans. The name's Montagu, by the way, Montagu Bunsen-Burner. What's yours?'

'John,' said the boy.

'What are you crying about, John?'

'I'm lost,' said the boy. He shivered. 'And I'm cold,' he said.

'Cold, eh?' said Montagu. 'That's easily remedied,' and he opened his jaws and carefully breathed long, slow, warm breaths at the child.

'Better?' he said.

'Oh yes, thank you,' said John. 'That's lovely!'

He stared at Montagu with great interest.

'I've never seen one before,' he said, 'but I think you must be a dragon.'

'Verily!' said Montagu. 'And not any ordinary old dragon either, I may tell you. The Bunsen-Burners are one of the oldest dragon families in Mercia – in the whole of Merrie England for that matter. Actually my wife's people are equally well bred – she was a Flame-Thrower, you know. Between us, we represent the very flower of dragonhood.'

'Oh,' said John. 'Have you any children?'

'Alas, no,' said Montagu sadly. 'Albertina has laid many eggs in her time, but none has ever hatched. I fear I am never to be a father nor she a mother.'

At these last words the boy's face fell.

'I have no mother,' he said. 'She died when I was but two years of age.'

'Oh dear,' said Montagu. 'How old are you now?'

'Seven.'

'So you live with your father?'

The boy gulped, and his eyes filled with tears once more.

'I did,' he said. 'My father is . . . was a woodcutter, but a great tree that he was throwing fell wrongly and crushed him, not a sennight since. And now I am alone, with no roof over my head and naught to eat but berries and nuts.'

Listening to this chapter of woe, Montagu Bunsen-Burner felt a strange sensation that he had never before felt in all his life. He could not have put a name to it, for dragons are in general merciless creatures, but in fact it was pity.

'Listen, little John,' he said. 'Why don't you come home with me? Albertina will be pleased to see you, I'm sure,' (because it'll show her I'm sticking to my diet, he thought) 'and at least you'll be warm and well fed, and you won't be alone any more.'

'You are kind,' said John.

He looked at the dragon and managed a smile, and then by chance he said exactly the right thing.

'Pray do not think me rude for smiling at you,' he said, 'but I had not thought that any creature could look as you do.'

'And how do I look?' said Montagu.

'Why, ugly!' said John, laughing now. 'You must be the ugliest animal in the world!'

At this Montagu threw back his head and gave a fiery snort of pleasure that turned a great patch of the oak leaves above brown and crackling.

'My boy,' he said, 'I can see that you and I are going to get on like a house on fire!'

2

Nothing Left to Lose

John never forgot the thrills of that first flight.

'Hop on my back,' Montagu said, and he laid himself down spatchcock, to make the climb up his side easier for the boy.

At first John looked doubtfully up at the mottled flank, red, green and yellow all mixed, that towered above him like a mountainside. But then he saw that the dragon's hide was covered with warty bumps, each the size of an anthill, and by using these as steps he clambered up quite easily. Beneath his hands and his bare feet, the dragon's skin felt dry and warm.

Montagu heaved himself upright.

'Ready for take-off?' he called.

'No! No!' cried John. 'Wait, Mr Dragon, please!'

'Call me Montagu.'

'Wait, Montagu!'

For I shall fall to my death, he thought, once we are aloft. There is nothing for me to hold on to.

Then he saw that, along the crest of the dragon's back, a whole row of thick, zigzag, triangular fins stuck up, the notch between each exactly of a size to make a saddle for a boy. He jammed himself between one zig and the next zag, and sat there, a leg on either side, the smallest of jockeys upon the largest of steeds.

'Ready?' called Montagu once again, turning his head to look back.

John's heart was beating so fast with a mixture of excitement and fear that he couldn't find the breath to speak, so he simply nodded.

Then, just behind him, the leathery bat-wings unfolded and spread and started to beat, slowly at first and then faster, and the great dragon began to rise from the forest floor.

'We have lift-off!' shouted Montagu, and up they went, to tree-top height and then, higher, higher, till the vast sprawling greenwood was left far below.

All this time John had kept his eyes tight shut, but now, as he felt the upward movement change to a forward one, he opened them, just a fraction at first, and then wide, and he gave a cry of amazement. All his short life had been spent beneath the canopy of the forest trees, and now suddenly here he was, miles above them it seemed, so that they looked like nothing so much as a great green meadow, with here a blue winding thread that was a river, and there a grey huddle that marked a village, while far below him birds wheeled and circled.

'Oh! Oh!' cried John at the sheer delight of flying, and 'Are you all right?' called Montagu.

'Yes, Montagu, yes!' shouted John. 'Oh, this is wonderful!'

Gone was all fear of falling, forgotten all the troubles of this ragged, hungry orphan. He was the lord of the sky, the ruler of the air, the monarch of all he surveyed!

'Faster, Montagu! Faster!' he cried, and for a while the bat-wings quickened. Then suddenly they clapped shut as the dragon set himself into a dive.

Always John was to remember the feelings that swept over him as they plunged earthwards − of surprise at the suddenness of the dive, then of shock at the speed of it, then of horror at the certainty that the dragon was bent upon killing them both, that he could

never pull out in time, that they must smash head-
long into the ground. Especially he never forgot how,
a few seconds later, his terror changed to a wonderful
warm sensation of relief and thankfulness and joy, as
Montagu spread his wings once more and levelled
out and glided, losing height and speed all the while
as the blessed earth came gently up to meet them. It
would be an exaggeration to say that the landing
was as light as a feather, but for a ten-ton dragon it
was a smooth job.

John wriggled out of his saddle and climbed down
the warty steps to the ground. They were in an
upland field, he could see, that was bounded at one
end by a rocky cliff. In the face of the cliff was the

black mouth of a cave. Montagu Bunsen-Burner began to make his way towards it.

'East, west, home's best!' he said. 'Come and meet my wife.'

But before they reached the cave mouth, a number of things came flying suddenly out of it, and as they drew nearer, John could see what they were. Bones! Thigh bones there were, and shoulder-blades, and rib-cages, and skulls, and most of them, by their size, seemed to have once belonged to large animals. But there were smaller bones as well, and among them a sword or two, some shields, a number of lances, and a plumed knight's helmet. This rain of objects was accompanied by huge clouds of dust, and when at last the fusillade ceased, John could hear within the cave a roaring, hissing sound and could see through the dust vivid flashes of flame.

'Od's bodkins!' said Montagu. 'I quite forgot! She did tell me, but it went right out of my mind. We'd have done better to stay away.'

'Why, what's happening?' asked John anxiously.

'Spring-cleaning,' said Montagu. 'She gives the place a thorough turn-out, chucks out all the rubbish and sweeps the floor with her tail. Then she burns off all the walls.'

'Why?'

'To kill off the bats and the bugs and the beetles and the fleas and the flies and such unwelcome visitors. Ever so house-proud Albertina is. All the

Flame-Throwers are the same.'

Shall I be an unwelcome visitor? John was thinking, when Mrs Bunsen-Burner stuck her head out of the cave mouth. Thin spirals of smoke still curled from her nostrils.

'Montagu!' she called in a voice that did not sound best pleased. 'Why are you home so early? I distinctly told you that I do not want you under my feet today.'

'I'm sorry, dear,' said Montagu. 'I forgot. It was finding this boy that put it out of my head.'

'Boy?' said Mrs Bunsen-Burner.

She came out of the cave and advanced towards them. She was almost as big as Montagu, John could see, but with nothing like as kind an expression.

'Yes,' said Montagu. 'I found him, so I brought him home.'

'Well, you can take him back again,' said his wife. '"No humans" I said, and "No humans" I meant, and it's no use telling me you just wanted a snack.'

She looked consideringly at John standing at her husband's elbow, and just about the height of it.

'On second thoughts,' she said, 'and talking of snacks, all that housework has made me quite peckish. I could do with a titbit. Leave him with me.'

'Albertina!' cried Montagu. 'You couldn't!'

'I could,' said Mrs Bunsen-Burner. 'You may be on a diet, Montagu, but I am not. Come here, boy.'

'Wait, wait, my dear,' said Montagu. 'He is an

21

orphan, poor little fellow – he has neither father nor mother. He was wandering in the forest, living upon berries and nuts. He is hungry.'

'He's not the only one,' said Mrs Bunsen-Burner. 'Move out of the way, Montagu, and let me get a clear shot at him.'

To face certain death without flinching calls for the greatest bravery of all, but maybe it helps if you have nothing left to lose.

Without parents, without a home, without even, it seemed, the support of his new-found friend Montagu against this harsh wife of his, John had nothing but his courage, and it did not fail him.

He walked straight towards Albertina Bunsen-Burner and stood directly in front of her, his hands on his hips. Cornflower-blue eyes stared up into eyes as red as the setting sun.

'Before you fry me,' said little John, loudly and clearly, 'I should like to tell you something. Which is this. It's a good job you never had any children.'

A short silence followed this speech.

Montagu held his breath.

John held his ground.

Albertina held her fire.

Then 'Why?' she said, very softly.

'Because,' said John, 'you are simply a big bully, about as hard and cold and cruel as your husband is kind and warm and friendly, and I would feel nothing but pity for any child that was unlucky enough to have you as a mother. You'd make a *pretty* mother, you would!'

There was a longer silence, broken only by a kind of gulping noise from Montagu, who could hold his breath no longer, while still the boy stood staring steadily at the she-dragon.

Then Albertina Bunsen-Burner took a

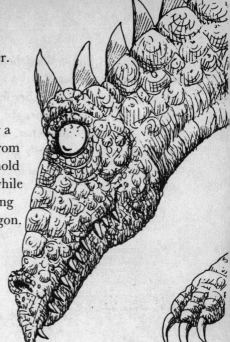

deep, deep breath, and Montagu, fearing the worst, exclaimed, 'No, Hotlips, no!'

But all that came from his wife's mouth was a long smokeless sigh, and then she turned away. As she did so, John could see, a single teardrop the size of a pumpkin ran slowly down the side of her repulsive face. She walked heavily back to the cave mouth and disappeared.

'I'm afraid I have hurt her feelings,' said John.

Montagu looked admiringly at him.

'You certainly gave her a mouthful,' he said. 'Which reminds me – let's go and get something to eat.'

3

'Don't Swallow It Whole!'

'Zounds!' cried John. 'I've never eaten so much in my life.'

His stomach was blown out like a little drum as he lay propped against the dragon's side. Bending his long neck in a U, Montagu had turned his head to face the boy, and his breath was pleasantly warm, if a trifle meaty.

'It's good stuff, is venison,' he said. 'Specially a tender young calf like we've just had. Lightly grilled, of course – it doesn't want to be overcooked.'

'Won't you get into trouble though, Montagu?' John said. 'The red deer of the forest are Royal game, Father told me. On penalty of death, none but the King of England may hunt them.'

'The King and I,' said Montagu lazily. 'What's his is mine, what's mine's me own.'

John thought about this for a while, and then he said, 'Montagu?'

'Yes?'

'You eat knights, don't you?'

'Yes, of course. That's to say, I used to, but now

I'm on this confounded diet.'

'Did you use to eat common folk too?'

'Certainly.'

'Suppose you had met the King, out hunting?'

'Don't suppose he'd have tasted much different.'

'So you eat anyone and everyone?'

'Of a surety.'

'Me?'

'Oh no, John, no, John, no!' said Montagu. 'Rest assured, no dragon will eat you.'

'What about your wife?' said John. 'She was all ready to make a meal of me.'

'H'm, yes,' said Montagu. He looked somewhat embarrassed. 'It would have been a slip of the tongue,' he said. 'Spring-cleaning tends to make her tetchy.'

'Will she have finished it when we get back?' asked John.

'Ah,' said Montagu. 'I see what you're driving at. All that housework will have made her very hungry. She will need something substantial.'

'Like a king-sized stag,' said John.

'Good thinking.'

So it was that when, late that day, Mrs Bunsen-Burner had at last scoured each crack and cranny and crevice of the cave, and made her weary way out of its mouth into the evening sunlight, she found what every housewife dreams of finding. Her husband was cooking the dinner.

The most delicious smells reached her soup-plate-sized nostrils, wafting up from the bottom of the field where she could see Montagu at work, on their picnic area. This was a flat outcrop of rock, a working-surface that allowed the dragons to cook without setting the forest afire.

Their cooking was primitive in the extreme. It consisted simply of placing the kill – a wild boar, for example – on the slab of stone, and then directing a jet of flame at it. Thus the outside of the animal would be charred and black, the inside raw; but the dragons' digestive juices were strong, and they were accustomed to bolting their food without much thought as to its flavour.

Now, however, the scent that reached Albertina was not the usual one of a burnt offering. It was a rich savoury scent that set her mouth watering, and mixed in with it was another smell, a pungent and unfamiliar one. Whatever was Montagu up to?

As she drew near, she could see that, in fact, there were two cooks at work, and that the meat was being prepared in what was literally a revolutionary fashion.

On a long lance suspended horizontally between two forked sticks, a great haunch of venison had been impaled, upon which Montagu was directing a steady but moderate flame. At the same time the boy was, with the point of a sword, turning the meat upon this spit, rotating it so that all was cooking

evenly. The fat meanwhile dripped down into the hollow of a knight's breastplate laid below.

As Albertina watched, Montagu ceased fire, whereupon the boy, using a skull as a rough ladle, scooped up some of the fat and dripped it carefully out of the eye-sockets on to the meat as it turned on the spit.

Montagu caught sight of his wife.

'Nearly ready, dear!' he called. 'A special dish, all for you, after your spring-cleaning. Smells good, doesn't it?'

'It does,' said Mrs Bunsen-Burner. 'What is it?'

'Deer, dear.'

'And what is the boy doing?'

'Tell her, John,' said Montagu.

'If it please you, ma'am,' said John, 'I'm basting it.'

'Basting? What is that?'

'Well, to baste is to drop fat over a joint while you are roasting it. It helps the meat cook right through evenly and stops it drying out, and it brings out the flavour.'

'Where did you learn this, boy?' asked Albertina.

'From my father, ma'am. Though 'twas rabbit, not venison.'

'A little more heat, John?' asked Montagu.

'Yes, please, Montagu.'

'Mr Bunsen-Burner, *if* you please!' said Albertina sharply.

'No, no, it's all right, Hotlips, my love,' said Montagu quickly. 'I told the lad he might address me so.'

He directed a final jet of flame at the haunch, and then, while John was pouring the last of the fat over the meat, spoke quietly into his wife's ear.

'He is a remarkable little boy, Hotlips, I do assure you. Young he may be, but he is wise in the lore of the forest. Why, already he has taught me a number of things, even as we journeyed back here after killing the stag.'

'Before you say anything else,' interrupted his wife. 'Where is the rest of the carcass? I see only one

30

haunch here. Do not tell me you have made a beast of yourself, Montagu!'

'No, no, dear, indeed not. The remainder of the animal is hanging up in a tree. I wedged the antlers between a fork at John's suggestion. He tells me that the meat will have even more flavour if it is hung for a number of days. Already he has pointed out to me all kinds of different fungi and herbs, which I sampled and found exceedingly tasty. Many can be used in cooking, he tells me – perhaps even now you notice an unusual smell?'

'I do. What is it?'

'Garlic, it is called,' said Montagu. 'The boy found some growing wild and rubbed the joint all over with it. Once again, it enhances the taste, so he tells me. I feel sure he will make himself most useful. He is a little treasure.'

'He'll be a little cinder if that meat's not ready soon,' said Albertina. 'All this cookery talk is making me ravenous.'

'Ready now, Mrs Bunsen-Burner,' said John. 'It's scalding, mind.'

'Scalding?' said Albertina. 'Stupid boy, dragons have fireproof throats,' and she pulled the haunch of venison off the spit.

'Please, ma'am!' cried John. 'Don't swallow it whole! Chew it a while, to get the beauty of it hot.'

They watched as Albertina chumped and swallowed and licked her hot lips, and chumped and swallowed again. Then, the meat gone, she put a paw to her mouth and drew out the thighbone and cracked it, licking out the marrow.

'How was it, dearest?' asked Montagu anxiously.

'Did you enjoy it, Mrs Bunsen-Burner?' asked John.

Albertina gave the most enormous belch.

'Boy,' she said, 'that was absolutely scrummy. You may call me Albertina.'

4

Why Not Dragons?

'Albertina,' said John.

'What is it, boy?'

Some months had gone by, months during which the two dragons had provided John with food, sheltered him, kept him warm of nights and stood ready to protect him from the dangers of the forest. In short, they had adopted him.

Now, Montagu had flown off hunting, and Albertina and John were going for a walk together. Or rather Albertina was walking and John was riding, comfortably sandwiched between two of her dorsal fins.

'I've been trying to say it for a long time,' said John.

'Say what?'

'That I'm sorry.'

'What for?'

'For being so nasty to you when we first met. I said a horrible thing – that it was a good job you hadn't had any children. Don't you remember?'

'I remember, boy,' said Albertina.

'Well, I'm very sorry, truly I am. Will you forgive me?'

'I'll consider the matter,' said Albertina.

By now John was used to the she-dragon's brusque manner of speech, and he knew that what she really meant was, 'I will'. He had also become quite accustomed to the fact that, for a dragon, 'ugly' = 'beautiful', and vice versa.

'Oh, thank, you, Albertina!' he said. 'You and Montagu are the ugliest dragons in the world! It's such a shame you never had a child. He or she would have been even more repulsive-looking.'

Albertina did not answer, and John wondered if he had overstepped the mark by mentioning such a thing. He tried to make amends.

'Anyway,' he said, 'it's lovely that you're such a happy couple. Have you been married long?'

'Fifty years,' said Albertina.

'Oh,' said John.

She must have laid a good few eggs in that time, he thought. Wonder why they never hatched? Perhaps now her egg-laying days are past.

'How long do dragons live?' he said.

'Couple of hundred years.'

Maybe there's hope yet, thought John. He cast about for a way of finding out what he wanted to know.

'How big is a dragon's egg?' he asked.

'About as big as your head,' said Albertina, 'which I shall shortly bite off if you keep asking silly questions. Mind your own business, boy.'

After that the rest of the walk was conducted in silence, and it was not until they were back at the cave and John had dismounted that Albertina spoke again.

'Look, boy,' she said, 'I know what you're after. You want to know why no egg of mine has ever hatched, don't you?'

John nodded.

'Well, I can't tell you,' said Albertina, 'because I don't know. I only wish I did. And, by the way, it's my turn to be sorry – for snapping at you. I tend to get a bit short-tempered at this time of year.'

'Why, what happens at this time of year?'

'I lay my annual eggs,' said Albertina.

'Where?'

'Here, in the cave, of course.'

Before John could comment on this, they heard the swoosh of Montagu coming in to land and heard his voice, and they went out to find him with a small bullock in his jaws.

'A nice piece of beef!' said Albertina with satisfaction. 'Well done, Monty! Now then, boy, go and see if you can get some of that hot root you found last time we had beef.'

'Horse-radish, d'you mean?' said John.

'That's it. And some seeds from that yellow plant, what d'you call it?'

'Mustard.'

'Yes. Off you go. We'll start the cooking.'

So it was not till much later, after there was nothing left of the bullock but a pair of horns and a tail-tuft and John himself was comfortably full of fillet steak (medium rare) that he had time to reflect upon what Albertina had said.

She laid her eggs in the cave.

What then?

John knew about eggs, for in the days – long ago now, it seemed – before the tree had killed his father, they had kept a few hens in the clearing round their little hut, and of course every one of the wild birds of the forest, from the proud, strutting pheasant to the perky little wren, acted in the same way.

To hatch their eggs, they sat upon them. Warmth, constant warmth over many, many days, was what eggs needed for the germ within to grow into a fully formed chick and then to chip its way out of the shell.

Surely to goodness Albertina did not sit upon her eggs?

Later that evening he managed to speak to Montagu alone.

'Montagu,' he said. 'Do you remember you told me once that your wife had laid lots of eggs, but none had ever hatched?'

'I remember, John, dear boy. A great sadness it has been to us, each year that passes. Come to think of it, it's about time she laid this season's clutch.'

'How many, as a rule?'

'About ten.'

'Where?'

'In the cave.'

'Surely,' said John, 'she does not sit upon them?'

Montagu threw back his head and let out such a hot roar of laughter that a passing woodpigeon fell to the ground oven-ready.

'Sit on them!' he hooted. 'Why, that would mean about a ton weight on each egg! No, no, she does not sit *on* them, she sits *beside* them.'

'Why?'

'To guard them, of course, from all the forest creatures that might fancy a dragon's egg for breakfast – wolves, bears, wild boar, even some of the larger birds.'

'And when they do not hatch?'

Montagu sighed deeply.

'That's the tragedy of it,' he said. 'Heart-breaking, it is. Comes the day when she says to me, "It's no use, Monty. There's no sign of life from them," and she walks out of the cave with the tears running down her hideous face, knowing she'll never see them again.'

'Why? What happens to them?'

'I get rid of them,' said Montagu. 'I dump them somewhere. The animals get them in the end.'

They don't *know*, thought John as he lay sleepless between the two great dragons that night, they just don't know that eggs have to be incubated! Their

mothers and fathers never told them, I suppose – no
wonder dragons are getting scarce in England now-
adays. So what's to be done? How can you hatch an
egg *without* sitting on it?

And then suddenly he had an idea.

He remembered how, a year or more ago, he had
been playing in the little bit of garden that his father
had dug out of the forest mould. In one corner had
been a green mound of vegetable leaves and weeds

and grasses – garden rubbish that his father had piled there. And he had put his hand into this heap. And it had been hot! Then he had scraped a crater in the top, so that steam rose into the air, and suddenly there in the warmth was a string of little eggs, perhaps forty of them, equal-ended ovals with a tough shell like parchment, all as warm as toast within the fermenting greenstuff.

When John had covered them up again and told his father, he'd learned that they were the eggs of a grass snake. A few days later he had opened the heap again, to find that the babies had hatched and gone. Only the broken egg-cases were left.

If snakes could hatch like that, why not dragons?

5

'There Are Nine Eggs'

John woke next morning with a racing brain. There were so many questions to be answered.

When would Albertina start laying?

How many eggs would she lay?

Would she lay them all in a week – a day – an hour?

Would each be, as she had said, as big as his head?

Supposing they were, and supposing she laid ten as Montagu had said she usually did, how ever could he, John, collect a large enough mound of greenstuff to act as an incubator for such a clutch?

And what would the dragons, Albertina in particular, think if they knew of his intentions?

After all, thought John, I may be quite wrong. Maybe dragons' eggs are different from snakes' eggs – perhaps they need to be laid in water, like frog-spawn, and heat would just kill them, so that they ended up as ten boiled dragons' eggs. I'd be popular then, wouldn't I?

What am I to do? One thing's certain – I must

keep my plan a secret.

At this point in his musings he felt Albertina stir, the signal for him to make a rapid exit from his bed and out of the cave; the dragons' waking involved a good deal of stretching and yawning, liable to over-lay or overheat a small boy.

This morning, however, Albertina snapped into action.

'Monty!' she said loudly. 'Get up!'

'Wassmarrer?' said her husband.

'Montagu!' said Albertina. 'Get up immediately, and go and have your bath. And take the boy with you.'

Montagu heaved himself to his feet, bumping his head on the roof of the cave as he always did, and looked, bleary-eyed, at his wife.

'What's the hurry?' he asked.

'Can you not guess?' said Albertina furiously be-tween clenched teeth. 'Take that pretty look off your face and go. I want to be alone.'

Not far from the dragons' cave – a little way beyond the picnic area in fact – there was a smallish lake which provided them with drinking water. It was just the right size for them to use as a swimming-pool, and every morning, winter or summer, they did their sixty lengths.

Between them, they had taught John to swim, first urging him to watch the action of the local frogs, and then taking him out on their backs into deep water; here they would gradually, day by day, sink a little lower under him, until one fine morning he managed half a dozen strokes by himself. From then on he made rapid progress, and before long he was using them as diving-rafts.

Now John paddled happily until Montagu had finished his stint. Then he climbed up the wet, mottled back and sat on a wart and looked around. Now that the dragon was still and the surface of the lake had calmed down, all the water birds – ducks, moorhens, coot and dabchicks – came out of the reeds.

Reeds! There's the greenstuff for my incubator, thought John. Masses of them, easy to pull out, all thick and wet and slimy, they'd heat up like anything! But he'd still need an enormous amount – it would take him ages to collect.

'Montagu,' he said, 'd'you think Albertina will lay her eggs soon?'

Montagu put his head under and blew, so that the water before his snout boiled and steamed. Then he raised it and shook the wet from it.

'I shouldn't be surprised,' he said drily.

'Perhaps this time they'll hatch,' said John daringly.

'If only they would,' said Montagu. 'If only *one* would – that's all I ask.'

Only one, thought John. That's it! That way I

needn't build as big a mound, and if it doesn't work, they may never know. Somehow I must steal a single egg from the clutch – with luck they won't notice just one missing. Oh, I wish she'd get on and lay them!

'Can we go home now, Montagu?' he said. 'Come on, I'm hungry.'

The dragons' first meal of the day was what you might call the full English breakfast, and because John could not manage the huge hunks of meat which they downed, Mrs Bunsen-Burner usually spoiled him with a nice fry-up which she cooked specially using a knight's shield as a frying-pan. Kidneys or a piece of liver – from deer or wild pig, ox or sheep – with perhaps a couple of duck eggs on the side went down a treat after his bathe.

'Come on,' he said again, but Montagu seemed in no hurry.

'We must wait awhile, John,' he said, looking at the sun to mark how far it had risen. 'Why not have a bit of diving practice first?'

He knew that the boy would not be able to resist this suggestion – the whole business was such fun.

The flat top of the dragon's head formed a diving-platform which could be lowered, quite close to the surface, or raised to full stretch to make a high diving-board. Best of all perhaps was the springboard effect, where Montagu would hold his head at water-level and then, with a sudden flip of his neck, send the boy

43

flying up and away as though shot from a cannon.

Half an hour passed happily at this sport, and then Montagu said, 'I should think it will be all right to go home now.'

'Breakfast will be ready, d'you mean?' asked John, but Montagu only grunted, and there were no savoury smells or sizzling sounds as they approached the picnic area. Indeed there was no sign at all of Albertina.

'Is she having a lie-in?' asked John as they approached the cave mouth.

'A lay-in,' said Montagu, and he called into the darkness, 'Albertina, dear! May we come in?'

The voice that answered 'Yes' sounded to John a trifle feebler than usual, more muted, less fruity. There was a reason for this.

There were ten reasons for this, John saw, once his eyes had grown accustomed to the gloom. Albertina had laid her clutch!

'Oh, Hotlips, dearest!' said Montagu gently. 'Are you all right?'

'Tired, Monty, a little tired,' replied his wife, drawing a weary paw across her brow. 'The effort one has to make, you know, for each of them. It takes it out of one.'

'Perhaps this time,' said Montagu, 'at last it will all be worth it.'

'Perhaps,' said Albertina with a sigh. 'I shall sit by them, day and night, as I always have. I can do no more.'

But I can, thought John.

'They are . . .' he began, then checked in horror as he realized he had been about to say 'beautiful' and changed it in the nick of time to '. . . beautiless, quite beautiless. I have never seen such plain eggs.'

'It is kind of you to say so, boy,' replied Albertina.

'May I touch one?'

'By all means.'

Strangely, the texture of the outer covering was rather like that of the grass snake's eggs, tough and rubbery, quite different from the shell of a bird's egg. They were not joined in a string like the snake's but separate, and each was indeed about the size of his head. They were round too, quite round. If he could not carry one, it would roll.

He checked again that there were ten.

Then a thought struck him.

Had Albertina counted how many? Would she count? Could she count?

Even if she could and had, he could always pretend he'd made a mistake.

'Nine,' he said. 'There are nine eggs, Albertina.'

'Really?' said Albertina. She did not seem particularly interested.

'A goodly number, my dear,' said Montagu in a comforting voice. 'A magnificent effort indeed. Will you take a little nourishment now? You must keep your strength up, you know. Breakfast in bed, eh? I'll soon rustle up something tasty.'

'I might manage a mouthful or two,' said Albertina faintly.

'I'll be as quick as I can,' said Montagu.

I must be quick too, thought John. The eggs will be quite all right for a while – after all, no one is brooding them – but the incubator will take some

46

time to heat up. I must start collecting the reeds now.

'Could you tell Montagu when he comes back,' he said to Albertina, 'that I'm going down to the lake? Just in case he wonders where I am.'

'What for, boy?' said Albertina.

'I saw some mushrooms,' lied John quickly, 'on our way back from bathing. I'm just going to pick a few.'

Half-way to the lake he found what he was looking for, not mushrooms but a suitable place to build the incubator, too far from the cave for the dragons to notice, but near enough for him to transport the egg fairly easily. It was a grassy hollow, ringed, and thus hidden, by bushes, and to it he carried armful after

armful of reeds from the lakeside and built them into a domed mound as tall as himself.

He had at last completed this task when he heard a loud voice calling his name in an agitated manner, and ran homeward to find Montagu huffing and puffing about the field below the cave in a fine state of anxiety.

'Wherever have you been?' he called when he saw John. 'What have you been doing all this time?'

'Just playing,' said John.

'Playing by the lake?' said Montagu, and for once he sounded quite angry, more like his wife in fact. 'I'll thank you to be more careful in the future, John, and not go wandering off on your own like that.'

'I'm sorry, Montagu.'

'Yes, well, don't do it again. Come and have your breakfast now. Would you like a duck egg?'

'Yes, please,' said John.

But the egg I really want, he thought, is not a duck's to eat but a dragon's to hatch. How am I going to steal it without Albertina noticing? And then something that Montagu said gave him an idea.

'You don't want to go to the lake by yourself,' the dragon told him. 'It could be very dangerous. Bears come down there to drink, and wolves.'

Ah, thought John. Suppose I wait till Montagu is off hunting. Then all I have to do is lure Albertina out of the cave for a little while, just long enough for me to nip in and take an egg. And the best way to get her to come out would be to pretend that I'm in danger and to call for help. She wouldn't be able to resist coming to my rescue and that would leave the eggs unguarded. Suppose I was to cry 'Wolf!'

6

'Wolf!'

The mound of reeds heated very quickly.

A couple of days later John put his hand into the top of it and found it already warm.

Each morning now Montagu would relieve his wife of her guard duties for a while, so that she could stretch her legs and have a drink and something to eat. Then, when she returned to the cave, off he would fly on the day's hunting. Normally he did not return until midday – which should give me plenty of time, John said to himself, to carry out my plan.

Accordingly on the third day after the laying of the clutch, he waited till Albertina was back in the cave and Montagu had disappeared over the tree-tops, and then prepared for action.

The idea was this. He would hide among the tumble of rocks outside the cave mouth. Then he would cry, 'Wolf!' Albertina would come rushing out and, not seeing him anywhere, go dashing about the field looking for him. While she was doing this, he would nip in, grab an egg, bring it out, and hide it among the rocks. Last of all, once Albertina was settled back in the cave, he would somehow transport the egg to the incubator.

It was the kind of plan that is guaranteed to go wrong, and the first time he tried it, it did.

Hidden behind a boulder, John cried, 'Wolf!' He shouted it out at the top of his voice, screamed it really to make it sound as though he was terrified. 'Wolf! Wolf!' he yelled. 'Oh, Albertina, come quickly!'

Sure enough, in half a minute Albertina came lumbering out of the cave, already puffing smoke and flames, and rushed out into the field. She looked about her, calling, 'Boy! Boy! Where are you? Where's the wolf?' Then she moved down towards the picnic area. 'I'll fry it, see if I don't!' she shouted.

So far, so good. But then, just as John emerged from hiding to slip into the cave, Montagu came flying back and landed right beside him.

'What's going on?' he said. 'What is Albertina doing away from the eggs, and why is she in such a tizzy?'

'It was a wolf,' said John. 'I saw a wolf and I was scared, so I called for help.'

At this point Albertina came puffing back.

'Can't see any wolf,' she said.

'You frightened it away,' said John quickly. 'It ran for its life. It was scared to death of you.'

'I bet it was,' said Montagu.

'What are you doing back already, Montagu?' said his wife.

'I forgot to ask,' he said, 'what you would fancy for lunch, Hotlips, dearest. Beef? Pork? Lamb? Venison? Or horse perhaps? I have not had horse since that last knight.'

'Oh, make up your own mind!' snapped Albertina. 'I am far too busy to be bothered with such decisions. And as for you, boy, do not expect me to come running every time something frightens you. It was probably only a fox anyway,' and she disappeared into the cave in a huff.

Nevertheless, when, next day, John once again cried, 'Wolf!' Albertina acted just as before, only this time John was successful.

Once she was well clear of the cave, he darted in and, choosing an egg at random, quickly carried it out and hid it in the rock tumble.

Once again Albertina came back saying she had seen no wolf.

Once again John explained it had fled.

Once again the she-dragon, grumbling that he was imagining the whole thing, went back into the cave and settled down beside the remaining eggs.

John waited a while, and then he took the egg from its hiding-place. Getting it to the incubator was made a great deal easier by the bright idea of rolling it all the way down the field, so that half the

journey was accomplished without his having to carry it. And when he did have to, it proved surprisingly light and easy to handle.

Once through the ring of bushes and in the grassy clearing, John laid it down and began to scoop out a hollow in the now steaming dome of the reed-mound, scraping away until he had made a hole a little larger than his head. Into this he popped the dragon's egg, and covered it over once more with reeds. 'Now,' he said, 'there's nothing more I can do except to wish you the best of good fortune, O child of Albertina (née Flame-Thrower) and Montagu Bunsen-Burner. For their sakes, may you have a happy hatching, however long it takes.' Then he turned and began to make his way home.

For once, John's senses were not as alert as usual. Normally he was aware of everything around him in the forest. Every sound or smell or movement meant something to him, and he was on the watch for anything of interest – a bird's nest, a bee-swarm, a plant of use for flavouring or food, a rabbit crouched in the undergrowth that might fall to a well-aimed stone. And chiefly, of course, he was on the look-out for danger – from the fierce wild beasts of the woods.

But this morning he was so pleased with himself at the success of his plan, so full of thoughts about the baby dragon that might result from it, that he strode home, head in air, quite unaware that he was being followed.

Fifty yards behind him, the she-wolf slunk silently between the trees, her yellow eyes fixed on the boy ahead, her red tongue lolling. Her ribs showed through her grey coat, and beneath her belly hung a drooping row of dugs, showing that, in a den some-where, she had a litter of cubs. Most of the prey she caught – rabbits, squirrels, mice – went to feed them, and she herself was very hungry. She closed gradually on the boy, and by the time John reached the picnic area, the fifty-yard gap had shrunk to ten.

John came out into the field, still blissfully unaware of being hunted, and began to walk up towards the cave. The she-wolf checked for a moment, crouching low in the last of the cover. She did not fancy crossing the open land, lest the cave which she could now see should contain other humans, big ones, with bows and arrows. But her hunger was too much for her, and soon she gathered herself and charged.

John was half-way up the field when he heard her coming, and lucky it was for him. For at about that point stood a solitary tree, a squat stunted oak, and he ran, gasping with horror and panic, and scrambled wildly up into it.

'Wolf!' he cried for the third time. 'Albertina, help me, save me, there's a wolf, really there is!'

Inside the cave Albertina had been dozing beside the eggs. She had taken the trouble to count them and had found that, as John had said, there were nine. Now the sound of his mad yells reached her.

'That boy!' she said. 'All he ever does these days is cry "Wolf!" and every time it's a false alarm,' and she settled herself again.

The wolf meanwhile was making every effort to get at John. Again and again she leaped up the thick trunk of the oak, her claws scrabbling on the bark, her jaws clacking together, before falling back with angry growls. And all the while John continued to shout for help, but there was no response from Albertina. Instead, the noise he was making attracted the attention of someone else.

No sooner had he heaved a great sigh of relief to see the wolf suddenly break off her leaping and slink away to one side than he saw the reason why.

Lolloping up the field came a huge brown bear. It reached the oak and reared on to its hind legs and peered up at John with small greedy eyes.

'A bear!' cried John. 'A bear! Help! Help!'

'Makes a change, anyway,' said Albertina sleepily to herself.

The bear began to climb.

7

'You're a Brave One'

Montagu was on his way home with a dead lamb in his mouth.

It was a big fat lamb, almost the size of its mother, but nevertheless hardly enough to make a meal for two large dragons and a growing boy. So just to be on the safe side, and to spare her grief, Montagu had gobbled up the ewe before taking off for the return flight. It was quite a habit of his to indulge in a mid-morning snack. It meant that he could then just toy with his food at lunchtime.

'No, no,' he would say with a light laugh, 'no

more for me, thank you. The rest is all yours. Must watch the old waistline, you know,' hoping that Albertina would comment favourably upon his generosity and strong-mindedness, though she never did.

Also he found that a good substantial elevenses made it less likely that he would, in a forgetful moment, swallow the prey he was carrying back to his mate. These in-flight meals had happened on occasion, much to Albertina's fury.

But she will be pleased with me today, he thought as he flapped easily along – prime English lamb, with a touch of that excellent sauce that John makes from the wild mint plant.

Even as he thought of the boy, he heard his voice in the distance, calling wildly for help.

Montagu went into overdrive.

As he cleared the edge of the forest at top speed, he could see that the noise was coming from the oak tree half-way up the home field, and that the cause of it, apparently, was a wolf, sitting on its haunches a little way away.

Silly boy, thought Montagu, what's he making all that fuss about? Wolves can't climb trees. He opened his mouth to shout this piece of information to John, quite forgetting the animal he was carrying in his jaws, which then hurtled earthwards like a stone and struck the grey hunter fair and square. Thus for the first, and probably the only time in history, was a wolf slain by a lamb.

Only now as Montagu reached the oak could he
see the real state of affairs. Perched precariously
among the topmost twigs of the highest bough was
the boy, and just below him a bear. The bear could
climb no further — it knew that the thin branches
would not support its weight — but it was cunning
enough to realize that, though it could not go on up,
the boy could come down.

It began to shake John's bough to and fro, harder
and harder, whipping him from side to side and
threatening to send him flying to the ground at any
moment.

Montagu, unable to blast the bear for fear of frying
John as well, hovered undecidedly beside the tree-
top, and, at sight of him, the bear stopped shaking
the branch and began hastily to descend. It reached
the ground and galloped away down the field past
the bodies of wolf and lamb. But though a bear can
run faster than a man, it hasn't a hope against a
flying dragon.

Swooping after it, Montagu let out one long searing jet of flame, and in an instant a live brown bear became a dead black one that rolled the few remaining yards into the picnic area and finished up neatly on the stone slab, wholly lifeless and partly roasted.

'Can't say I've ever eaten one of these,' said Montagu later.

John had gathered some mint, and they had cooked the lamb and taken it up to Albertina, who had scoffed the lot.

Now they were wondering what to do about the carcass of the bear.

'My father told me once,' said John, 'that the hams of a bear are delicious. But they must be smoked, and then hung for a good while.'

'No problem about that,' said Montagu.

So between them – John using his spit-turning sword and Montagu his teeth – they got the skin off the bear, and cut off his hams, and then the dragon spent the afternoon blowing clouds of hot smoke over them. John meanwhile scraped the fat off the inside of the great hairy pelt and then pegged it out to dry, thinking it would make him the warmest of blankets in wintertime.

As they made their way back up to the cave, they could see that already the scavengers – buzzards, ravens and carrion crows – were busy about the body of the she-wolf. The birds flew away as they approached and now John saw what he had had no time or inclination to notice before.

'Look, Montagu!' he said. 'She's all milky. Our dog had puppies once and she looked just like that. She's got cubs somewhere, and now they'll probably starve to death.'

'Good,' said Montagu.

'Oh, Montagu, how can you say that! I wish I could find them, poor little things.'

During the next couple of days, John searched the length and breadth of the line of cliffs that stretched on either side of the dragons' cave. Some hole or cranny among the rocks, he reasoned, would be a likely place for a wolf's den. But he also explored a number of possible sites in the forest, keeping a sharp eye out for danger all the time.

On the second morning he happened to pass near to the reed-mound, and could not resist scraping away the top to have a look at the egg, now in its fifth day of incubation. It felt beautifully warm – just about the right temperature, it seemed to him.

By the third day after the death of the she-wolf, John had more or less given up hope of finding the cubs. He was sitting on the fallen trunk of a great beech tree that had been blown down by some winter gale, thinking that by now the wretched orphans must be dead. The forest was quite silent save for the distant tapping of a woodpecker. Suddenly, from somewhere under the maze of exposed roots at the base of the tree, the faintest whimper came to his ears.

In a flash he was off the trunk and down on his knees beside the tangle, to find, between two big roots, a deep hole. It was a wolf-sized hole, and from its depths there came once more a thin whining.

In his excitement it did not occur to John that this could be the den of another wolf, a live one, that might appear at any moment or indeed actually be inside the hole. He reached into the darkness within and felt about, till his hand touched something soft and furry. He pulled it out.

It was a dead cub, stiff and cold.

Again he felt about, and again, and brought out two more little grey bodies, but still he could hear the whimpering.

Once more John jammed himself down into the hole as far as his shoulders would allow and stretched out one arm to its fullest extent, and at last his hand touched something that moved, something alive, and he pulled the fourth wolf cub out into the light of day. Unlike its litter-mates, it was coal-black, he saw, and it stared back at him with baby-blue eyes.

It was very weak, at death's door, it seemed to John, but even so it bared its little milk-teeth and with the feeblest of growls snapped at his fingers.

'You're a brave one, you are,' said John, 'and I'll tell you something, my friend. I'm going to save your life, see if I don't.'

8

Bart

And save it he did, though it was not easy. Luckily John had a good deal of common sense for a boy of his age. He knew, for example, that *he* could not live on meat alone as the dragons did, and he was careful to take advantage of all the many items of food that the forest provided – the fruits, the nuts, the fungi and such tender young salad plants as dandelion and watercress.

Now, he realized straightaway that the black cub's immediate need was not for solid food, but for liquid of some kind. Starving hungry it might be, but it would also be dehydrated, three days after its last drink of its mother's milk. Its brothers and sister, he did not doubt, had died of thirst.

Carrying it, he ran as fast as he could to the lakeside. Here, gathering a handful of spongy moss, he soaked it in water which he squeezed into the cub's jaws, a little at a time. At first it resisted feebly, but then seemed to realize that he was trying to help it and began to swallow the water greedily.

'What can I give you to eat?' John mused. 'I

expect your mother swallowed what she killed and partly digested it and then sicked it up again for you. Well, I'm sorry, my friend, but I'm not going to do that. And yet it's no good offering you great chunks of meat such as the dragons eat – you need something tender and easy to digest. But what?'

Even as he asked the question, the answer jumped out of the lakeside reeds and splashed into the water. A frog. Frogs must be edible after all – he'd often watched the tall grey herons spearing them, and once he'd seen a swimming frog suddenly disappear with a plop and a swirl to make a meal for one of the lake's big pike.

He found a tussock of dry grass and laid the wolf cub in it, guessing, rightly, that it was too weak to make its escape, and then he went frog-hunting. There were plenty about, and it was not long before he returned with one. A tap on the head with a stick had killed it, and with a sharp-edged flint John cut off the plump upper part of one of its long legs and offered this to the cub. To his delight, the little animal began to worry at the meat, and managed before long to chew and swallow a mouthful.

From then on, the wolf cub seemed to grow stronger by the minute. The second drumstick went the way of the first, and off John went to hunt again. Frogs' legs, it seemed, were a delicacy. In the course of catching and killing another frog, he came upon a dabchick's nest in a floating tangle of water-weed; there were four white eggs in it, and he broke these for the orphan to lick up. It had just finished when suddenly it froze as a huge shadow swept over them.

'Don't worry,' said John, picking the cub up and cuddling it. 'It's only Montagu, coming for a swim,' and they watched as the dragon circled and dived and belly-flopped into the middle of the lake with a splash that sent great fountains of water high in the air.

'Montagu!' shouted John. 'Come and see what I've got!'

The dragon swam over, pushing a great wave before him so that John hastily had to retreat as though before an incoming tide.

'What is it?' said Montagu.

'A wolf cub!'

Ugh! What a pretty thing, thought Montagu disgustedly, but not wanting to hurt John's feelings, he said in a jolly voice, 'Well, well, what an ugly little creature!'

'What!' cried John. 'Oh. Yes. I was forgetting.'

'Is it a he or a she?'

'A he.'

'What d'you call it?'

'I haven't given him a name yet,' said John. 'You can help me choose if you like. Do you have any favourite ones?'

Montagu thought deeply. Never having had any children of his own, he was not practised in this sort of selection. But after a while he said, 'How about

Bartholomew Theophilus Marmaduke?'

'Why all those names?' said John.

'They were my father's.'

What awful names, thought John, but not wanting to hurt Montagu's feelings, he only said, 'They're very long.'

'Father was a very long dragon,' said Montagu.

'What did your mother call him?'

'Bart.'

'I like that,' John said, and he tickled the black cub under his chin. 'Come on, Bart,' he said. 'I must introduce you to Albertina.'

'Want to fly back?' said Montagu.

A good idea, thought John. That way we shan't have to walk up the field past what's left of Bart's mother.

'Yes, please,' he said, and he waded out carrying the cub, and climbed up the dragon's side into his usual seat. Whether it was because his eyesight was still babyish, or whether he was simply full-fed, Bart showed no fear as they took off, and indeed was fast asleep by the time they landed.

'Do you think,' said John, 'that you could go in and tell Albertina? About Bart, I mean. I don't want her frightening him, or worse, which she might if I take him inside without warning. He is a wolf after all, even though a very small one, and you know how protective she is of her eggs. Could you ask her nicely if I can bring him in?'

'Ask her nicely?' said Montagu. 'I shall tell her that you are bringing the creature in. To hear you talk, anyone would think I am not master in my own cave.'

The roar of rage that followed close upon Montagu's entry showed clearly that indeed he was not.

'What is this I hear?' cried Albertina, emerging from the cave with a look of deep disapproval on her face, followed by a crestfallen Montagu. 'Where is this beautiful little beast? A wolf indeed! I'll have no wolves in my cave, boy – let that be clearly understood. So you can just put it down on the ground this minute. I'll frizzle it, and that will be an end to the matter. Come along now. Do as you're told.'

'But, Hotlips, dearest . . .' began Montagu.

'But nothing,' said Albertina, 'and don't you "Hotlips" me. That pretty creature has got to go, d'you hear me, boy?'

'Yes,' said John. 'I hear you.'

He clutched the cub tightly, for it was shivering at the harsh tones of the she-dragon's voice.

'Now you hear me,' he said. 'This is my wolf cub. I found him. I rescued him. And I'm going to keep him. Here. In this cave. Which is my home as well as yours, you've always given me to understand, Albertina. I'm going in now. If you frizzle Bart, you frizzle me.'

For a moment it looked as if Albertina might. Her eyes glowed like red-hot coals and twin jets of smoke

spurted from her nostrils. Then she gave a snort of disgust.

'Oh, I can't be bothered to argue with you!' she said. 'Too cocky by half, you are – defying your elders and betters. It's all your fault, Montagu – you spoil the boy, you've no idea how to treat children, a fine father you'd have made.'

A fine father he still will make, I hope, thought John. I wish he'd stand up to her a bit more though.

But when Albertina continued, 'Go and guard the eggs, I'm going for a bathe,' Montagu meekly turned and disappeared into the cave.

As soon as Albertina was airborne, John put Bart down on the ground, and they watched the she-dragon winging away towards the lake.

'Tomorrow,' said John, 'we'll go down to the incubator and see if anything's happening. If only that egg will hatch! It would give them a whole new interest in life – a child would make such a difference to both of them, I'm sure. As for you, well, you have no mother or father, poor little chap, but you've got me.' He patted his new pet. 'Good wolf!' he said. 'Come along now,' and he walked into the cave.

Bart followed.

9

The Faintest Chirrup

In fact they did not visit the incubator next day, nor for a number of days after that. John's problem was threefold. He could not leave the cub alone with Albertina – he did not trust her. He did not want Bart to have to walk past his mother's remains. And anyway, thirdly, the distance to the incubator was too much for the little wolf's legs.

The only way for them to get to the lake, and from there to the reed-mound, was by air, and though Montagu was only too willing to oblige, he then always hung around after their bathe.

At first Bart was very worried to see his master splashing about some way from land, and he would stand at the brink, whining and howling. But gradually he grew used to the idea, and, what is more, strong enough to begin hunting on his own account, so that one morning a week later he caught a frog all by himself.

When another week had gone by, the change in the wolf cub was so marked that John felt it was time to try the journey on foot. Bart seemed almost to have doubled his size, and his black coat was glossy with health.

So one afternoon, while Montagu was still away hunting and Albertina was snoozing beside her cold clutch, they set off down the field. John was careful to keep away from the spot where the lamb had killed the wolf, but in fact by now there was nothing left to show what had happened but a few scattered, scentless bones.

At the picnic area Bart sniffed at the great pegged-out bearskin, and his little hackles rose.

'Just you remember that smell, Bart,' John said, 'and if you ever meet one of those in the forest, give it a wide berth. Come along now.'

Bart came along, instantly. His intelligence was extraordinary. John had thought that the wolf cub would, like a puppy, have to be taught to obey a number of commands, but there was no need. Bart seemed to anticipate anything that the boy might have required him to do.

Wherever John went, the cub followed hard on his heels, and when he stopped, Bart would lie down. He learned immediately, after one lesson, that the pressure of a hand on top of his black head meant 'Stay exactly where you are and don't move a muscle till you're told', and that a raised arm, if his master was in sight, or, if not, a shrill whistle, meant 'Now come to me'.

When they reached the incubator, John uncovered the dragon's egg once more. 'Nearly a month now,' he said to it, 'but you just look exactly the same to me. If only I could know whether anything is happening inside.'

Then he had a thought.

At home in the cave he had one day allowed Bart to have a look at the clutch. He had of course chosen a time when Albertina was out and Montagu, sitting in, was actually busy in a far corner doing a spot of housework on his wife's orders. The cub, however, had shown absolutely no interest in the nine eggs. Would it be the same with this one?

Beckoning Bart, he pointed, and the cub stood on his hind legs against the mound and put his nose against the tenth egg and sniffed at it.

Immediately his ears pricked, his tail began to wag, and he whined excitedly. 'There's something in there!' was what his every action said – of that there was no doubt in John's mind at all. Bart's senses were so much more acute than his own, and something – a scent, the faintest vibration or just plain instinct – had told him that there was life inside the rubbery shell.

In high excitement John piled the reeds back on top.

'Bart my lad,' he said, 'from now on we must come every day to inspect it. Just imagine if it should hatch out and then wander away and get lost or eaten by something. How terrible that would be!'

So it was with bated breath, each afternoon, that

John approached the reed-mound, hoping desperately that the baby would not have hatched and gone, yet disappointed every time to see that nothing further had happened. And nothing did, for a further endless two weeks, until one unforgettable day when Bart, having excitedly sniffed the uncovered egg as usual, put his black head on one side and laid an ear against the shell, listening intently. Then he looked up into John's face and positively grinned.

The message was plain and the boy in his turn bent and listened. From inside the egg came the faintest chirrup!

John and Bart stood and watched and waited tensely. The minutes passed and the chirrups grew stronger and more frequent. Then, after an hour, they heard a tapping sound and suddenly what looked like a tooth broke through the surface. In fact, that was exactly what it was – the egg-tooth, the hard point on the beak with which every bird or reptile breaks out of its prison, and in a moment it had enlarged the hole enough for the baby dragon to poke out its snout, and soon its whole head appeared.

It looked at boy and wolf cub with little ruby eyes.

'Daddy?' it said. 'Mummy?'

'No, no,' said John. 'I'm a boy called John and this is my wolf cub Bart.'

The baby dragon's face, which was already rather wrinkly, wrinkled some more, and its red eyes filled.

'Me got no daddy or mummy?' it asked in a quavery voice.

'No, no,' said John. 'I mean, yes, yes, you've got both of them, only they don't know about you yet. You're going to be a surprise, you see.'

The baby shook its head as though all this was too much for it.

'Look,' said John. 'Let's get you out of that egg and then I can explain. Here, I'll give you a hand,' and carefully he pulled and prised at the edges of the hole in the shell until it was big enough for the baby dragon to struggle through.

It was a perfect miniature of its parents, down to the last detail, and in colour a pale shade of green. Instinctively, John stretched out a hand to stroke it down its many-finned back, so pretty did it look. Just in time, he remembered correct dragon-talk.

'What a pre ... what an ugly boy you are!' he said admiringly.

'Me girl,' said the baby dragon simply.

'Oh, I beg your pardon!' said John. 'I mean, I didn't know.'

How does *she* know, he thought? Only just born and already she's sure she's female. Next thing, she'll be telling me her name.

'You John?' said the baby.

John nodded.

'You Bart?'

Bart wagged his tail.

The baby dragon opened her little mouth in what was quite obviously a smile of delight. She had a great many tiny teeth, John noticed, and her breath was already quite hot.

'Me lucky,' she said.

Does she mean that's what she's called, John wondered?

'Are you saying that your name is Lucky?' he asked.

'You like?'

'Oh yes, it's nice.'

'Then,' said the baby dragon, 'me Lucky.'

IO

'Me Lucky'

Montagu meanwhile was on his way back from hunting.

He had chanced upon a big bristly sow and her litter of eight young ones, and having first made a pig of himself by swallowing all the black-and-brown-striped babies – for streaky was his favourite kind – was now bringing home the bacon.

He landed and laid the body of the sow outside the cave, and called, 'Hotlips! I'm ba-ack!'

Receiving no reply, he made his way in, to find Albertina standing and gazing at the nine eggs. How amazingly hideous she is, he thought fondly. Why, she's ugly enough to turn milk sour!

'Dearest,' he said, 'I've brought you something really nice for supper.'

'I don't want anything to eat,' said his wife. 'I couldn't manage a mouthful.'

'Why, whatever's the matter?' said Montagu. 'You sound so unhappy.'

'I am,' said Albertina. 'Oh Monty, I am!'

'What is it? Tell me, dearest.'

'It's the eggs. It's just the same again. They're never going to hatch.'

'Oh, don't say that, Hotlips. They may – in a day or so.'

'No, Monty, no. Today is the day they should have hatched, don't ask me how I know, I just do, I feel it in my bones,' said Albertina.

Gently she touched the eggs with her snout.

'Farewell,' she said softly.

'You mean . . . ?' said Montagu.

'Yes,' said Albertina. 'Get rid of them. Take them hence to a place of your choosing and there surrender them to the tender mercies of the wild beasts of the forest. We are never to be parents, it seems.'

'Perhaps next time,' said Montagu.

'There may well not be a next time,' said Albertina heavily. 'I am not as young as I was.'

She moved slowly past her husband to the cave mouth. There she turned and gave one final look at the clutch.

'Dead!' she said. 'And never called me Mother.'

Then, with bowed head, she made her way out into the evening sunshine.

'Mummy?' said Lucky at about the same moment. 'Daddy? John take Lucky see Mummy and Daddy?'

She slid down the side of the reed-mound and stood beside Bart, looking up at the boy. Now it was possible to realize how very cramped her last days within the egg must have been, for she was already the size of a large, if short-legged, cat. John was ready in case Bart should go for her, but the wolf cub only sniffed at the baby dragon and then wagged his tail.

'Yes, of course,' John said. 'We'll go right away. It won't be too much for you though, will it? It's quite a long walk.'

'Walk?' said Lucky scornfully. 'Me fly!' and she stretched out a pair of tiny wings and flapped them like mad, but did not succeed in lifting herself even an inch from the ground.

'Methinks me not fly,' she said thoughtfully.

'I'd better carry you,' said John. 'I expect your wings will have to grow a bit first, and, anyway, you'll probably have to learn how. Albertina and Montagu will love to teach you.'

'Who they?' said Lucky.

'Those are the names of your mummy and daddy,' said John, and he explained to Lucky about the dragons' problems and the reasons why they had never before managed to have children.

'Me first baby?' said Lucky.

'Yes, the child of their old age,' said John. He picked the baby dragon up. 'Let's go,' he said. 'I can't wait to hear what Albertina says when she sees you.'

*

Albertina was walking slowly towards the lake. Her heart was very heavy. Something told her that her egg-laying days were finally over, that there would never be another chance. Adoption was all very well – John was a good boy really, and she supposed she'd have to put up with the wolf cub, seeing how fond he was of it – but if only she could have had a child of her own, just one, a girl preferably, a little green girl.

At that moment she saw the boy in the distance, coming towards her, the wolf at his heels. He seemed to be carrying something, but because Albertina's red eyes were swimming with self-pity (and, anyway, she was short-sighted to boot), she could not make out what it was.

'Pull yourself together,' she said. 'This is no way for a Bunsen-Burner to behave, much less a Flame-Thrower,' and she hastily wiped away her tears with a paw and sat down in a casual manner to await the boy's arrival. She was careful not to watch his approach, but looked away, at the trees, at the sky, at a flock of passing birds, the perfect picture of a dragon communing with nature, composing a little poem perhaps, a dragon who could not be less interested in whatever it was that the boy held in his arms.

Not till she heard him call her name would she turn her head, she decided, saying as she did so, 'Ah boy! How you startled me!' in an affected way. But she did not hear his now familiar voice saying 'Albertina.'

Instead she heard a voice that she had never heard before, a childish piping voice that uttered but one single word, the word for which she had waited so long.

'Mummy!' it said.

There was nothing affected about the great start of surprise that Albertina gave. Her eyes, it seemed to John, were liable to pop out of her head, and that usually commanding voice was muted as she stared at the creature that John had placed upon the ground before her.

'What did you say?' she whispered.

'Me said "Mummy",' replied Lucky. 'You my mother, me your daughter.'

There was a long silence. John waited, wreathed in smiles. By his side stood the wolf cub, tail waving, tongue lolling, a positive grin upon his face. As for Albertina, she was the very picture of a flabbergasted dragon.

'I don't understand,' she muttered. 'Montagu has taken the eggs away, all nine of them.'

She looked at her adopted son, and, for the first time ever, did not address him as 'boy'.

'John,' she said. 'How can this be a child of mine?'

'You laid ten eggs,' said John. 'I stole one,' and then he told her everything.

'They need constant heat, you see,' he finished. 'For six weeks. Just sitting beside them is no good.'

'To think!' said Albertina. 'I never knew. My parents never told me, you see, they did not think it nice to talk of such things. Oh, how happy I am! To have a girl, a little green girl! Wait till I tell Monty that he is a father. He will fly over the moon!'

'I'll send Bart to fetch him,' said John, and to the cub he said, 'Find Montagu. Good wolf!'

'Oh, John!' said Albertina, as Bart loped away, nose to ground, 'how clever you've been!'

'Me clever too,' said Lucky in a rather hurt voice.

'Of course you are, darling!' said Albertina. 'You're the cleverest little dragon in Merrie England, and the most ill-favoured. Why, your little face is as ugly as sin! Whatever shall we call you?'

'She's got a name already,' said John. 'She named herself.'

'What is it, darling?' asked Albertina.

'Me Lucky.'

'Lucky?' cried Albertina, reverting to her usual

braying tones. 'What does the child mean? One has never heard of such a name! She must mean Lucy.'

'No, Mummy,' said the child firmly. 'Lucky.'

'It's more of a nickname, I expect,' said John tactfully. 'You know, like your husband has a pet name for you.'

'Possibly,' said Albertina, 'but that is not good enough for a daughter of Montagu Bunsen-Burner Esquire and his wife Albertina (née Flame-Thrower). Mummy will decide what you are to be called, darling.'

Lucky pouted, and two tiny puffs of smoke came from her infant nostrils.

'No!' she said.

'Mummy knows best,' said Albertina, a shade less confidently.

'No!'

'Little dragons,' said Albertina, 'should be seen and not heard.'

'No, no, no!' said the little dragon. 'Me Lucky, you silly!'

That's taken the wind out of the old girl's sails, thought John. The husband may be henpecked, but the daughter's a proper little madam!

As for Albertina, she positively spluttered.

'Silly?' she said. '*Silly?* Just you wait until I tell your father. Never in my life have I been spoken to in that fashion!'

*

They had not long to wait, for, in fact, Bart had made short work of finding Montagu. Having ferried the nine discarded eggs to the dumping-place he usually used for this sad task, the dragon was also on his way to the lake, by air, to drown, not himself, but his sorrows in a long cold drink. A good swim, he thought, might help to wash away the sadness of having had, for the umpteenth time, to administer the last rites to yet more unborn children.

Suddenly he saw a black shape running across a clearing below him, and, diving down, recognized Bart and landed near by.

The cub, he could see immediately, was in a high state of excitement, jumping up at him and whining and yapping eagerly. Bart ran back a little way and returned again, and then repeated this behaviour until the dragon got the message. 'Follow me!' was what Bart was plainly saying, and Montagu did, blundering along through the forest in the wake of the hurrying cub.

Albertina is in trouble, he thought! Or John! If anyone's harmed a hair of their heads, he said to himself (quite forgetting that Albertina hadn't any), I'll fry 'em! And by the time he came in sight of his wife and the boy, he had worked himself up into a fine state of fury, roaring fit to shake the very trees and shooting out great gouts of flame that threatened to set them all ablaze.

At sight of this terrible monster approaching,

Lucky ran hastily to her mother and hid behind her huge body, crying, 'Mummy! Mummy! Save me!' upon which Albertina quite forgot her anger.

'It's all right, darling,' she said. 'It's only Daddy, playing games. Don't worry, Mummy will look after you.'

'What's up?' shouted Montagu as he drew near. 'Knights, is it? Where are they? I'll burn 'em, I'll bake 'em, I'll boil 'em! Blasted knights, that's what they'll be!'

'Calm down, Monty,' said Albertina, 'and cool down, do, or we'll have a forest fire. There's no need to get all hot and bothered, nothing nasty's happened. On the contrary, we've a lovely surprise for you, haven't we, John?'

'Yes, we have, Montagu,' said John, and Bart yapped with pleasure.

'Lovely surprise?' said Montagu. 'I can't see anything,' and nor he could for the baby was hidden by the mother's bulk.

'Well,' said Albertina, 'if you could have one wish granted, what would it be? Today, of all days.'

'Today, of all days?' said Montagu wearily. 'Ah, Hotlips, that's a hard thing to ask me, when you know the sad task in which I have just been engaged. Why do you make me play such games?'

'All right, Monty dearest,' said Albertina gently. 'Don't bother with the wish. Just say one word, will you? Just to please me?'

'One word? What?'

Albertina put her mouth to his ear and whispered.

'Say it nice and loud,' she added.

Montagu sighed. 'Oh, all right,' he answered. 'If I must,' and in a very bored voice he said, 'Lucky.'

Albertina rose and stood aside, to reveal what had been hidden behind her.

'Hello, Daddy dear,' said Lucky Bunsen-Burner.

'Very High Marks'

To John time seemed to fly, after the hatching of the baby dragon.

The days and weeks sped by, and before you could look round, the moon had waxed and waned twelve times, and Lucky's first birthday was almost upon them.

John had grown a couple of inches in that year, and as for Bart, though he was still leggy and had not yet filled out fully, he was as tall as an adult wolf.

But of course it was Lucky who had altered out of all recognition, as you must do if you weigh nine or ten pounds at birth and aim to finish up at nine or ten tons. Now her head was on a level with John's, and her green body was the size of a cow's.

Before that though, while she was still only six months old, time was not the only thing that had flown. So, after a course of lessons from her father, had she.

John had been right – her wings needed to mature, and at first they were not strong enough to lift her.

Montagu, as one would have guessed, was totally besotted by his daughter and spoiled her rotten. This is not to belittle Albertina's feelings, which were equally deep, but the responsibility of discipline and of the proper upbringing of the child fell squarely upon her, and indeed by her very nature, she welcomed it.

So it was to her father that Lucky turned whenever she wanted her own way, knowing full well that she could wheedle anything out of him, and (in a manner of speaking, since she hadn't one) twist him round her little finger. When it came to the question of flying, however, she found to her surprise that for once she could not move him.

'I'm sorry, sweetheart,' said Montagu, 'but I'm not having you just taking off into the wild blue yonder. You are a learner-flyer, and you are going to have a proper course of flying lessons from a proper instructor – me.'

'But I don't want to, Daddy,' said Lucky. 'Flying's easy, I'm sure. I don't want silly old lessons. I don't have to, do I, Daddy darling?'

'Yes,' said Montagu firmly. 'You do. Air safety is very important. Accidents can only too easily happen, especially at take-off and landing, the most risky parts of any flight, and there is a great deal to learn about the Airway Code. Daddy's going to teach his little girl to fly properly.'

Lucky then tried to enlist her mother's support.

'Mummy,' she said. 'Daddy's saying I've got to have flying lessons.'

'Quite right,' said Albertina.

'But I don't want to. I can learn to fly by myself.'

'Your father's word is law,' said Albertina. 'Whatever he tells you to do, you will do it.'

'You don't,' said Lucky cheekily.

'Luck-y!' said Albertina on a rising note, and Lucky beat a hasty retreat, fearing a good hard slap from her mother's tail.

In fact the flying lessons, when they began, turned out to be brilliant. Montagu was the most patient of instructors, and never spoke sharply to his daughter (as Albertina would have done) if she made mistakes, such as giving a wrong paw-signal or braking too suddenly. Slowly and carefully he took her through the whole range of necessary aerial skills – the three-point turn, the emergency stop, the controlled stall, the side-slip, and, as the lessons progressed, he taught her such aerobatics as looping the loop, the 'falling leaf' and the 'victory roll'.

'And always,' he would say, 'remember your undercarriage, sweetheart. Raise it on take-off, lower it before touchdown. Except on water, of course. There you can do a pancake landing – it's fun.'

And it was, it all was.

After twelve lessons, Montagu judged that it was time for Lucky to take her test. He flew off one morning to make the necessary arrangements with

the Examiner, an elderly and much-respected dragon who lived by himself (he was a widower) on the far side of the great forest.

'Tomorrow,' he said to Lucky on his return. 'He's coming tomorrow, so it's early bed for you tonight, sweetheart. No need to be nervous – the old boy's very fair – but I think I'd better give you a few tips. First, speak up nice and loud when he asks you questions, he's a bit deaf. Second, don't go buzzing about the sky at top speed because he's not as nippy as he was, and if he can't keep up with you, he's liable to fail you out of pique. And third, always call him "sir".'

'All right, Daddy,' said Lucky. 'It'll be a piece of cake.'

Next morning the Examiner, an elderly, rather thin grey dragon, arrived. He hovered above the oak tree near the cave and called in a querulous, high-pitched voice, 'Miss Bunsen-Burner! Scramble, if you please!'

'Coming, sir!' cried Lucky, and she took off and rose to join him.

Montagu and his wife and John and his wolf gazed

up into a clear blue sky as the Examiner proceeded to put the learner-flyer through her paces.

'What are her chances, d'you think, Monty?' asked Albertina anxiously.

'Hopefully she will pass first time,' said Montagu.

'She's good,' said John. 'You watch.'

And, indeed, as they did, it seemed she was.

Every manoeuvre was promptly and neatly executed, and all the time they could see that Lucky was being careful to keep her air speed low.

Eventually both dragons came in to land, wings spread wide to act as air brakes, and came to a halt before the watchers, feet and tail touching down in a perfect five-point landing.

'Ah, good morning, Bunsen-Burner,' panted the Examiner.

Courteously, he bowed his hoary head towards Albertina.

'Mrs Bunsen-Burner,' he said.

He cast a curious eye upon John and Bart, but made no comment.

They waited until he had got his breath back.

'Well, sir?' said Montagu.

'High marks,' said the Examiner. 'Very high marks. How I wish that all the youngsters who come before me were as steady and sensible. I have no hesitation in passing your daughter.'

He turned to Lucky.

'Congratulations, young lady,' he said. 'You are now a Fully Qualified Licensed Flying Dragon.'

Later, when the Examiner had taken a little refreshment and said his goodbyes and gone, Montagu and Lucky took off together in celebration.

They climbed steeply, and then proceeded to fly off in opposite directions until they were about a mile apart. Here they turned.

What they were about to demonstrate, though the three on the ground did not know it, was the Mid-

Air Collision Avoidance Procedure, and now they started to fly straight at one another at maximum speed.

A head-on collision seemed inevitable.

'No! No!' cried Albertina and John with one voice, and Bart pointed his nose at the heavens and howled the wolf's long, mournful howl. But at the very last moment, Lucky obeyed that rule of the code that says 'in the event of possible mid-air collision, turn always to starboard', and she slid neatly down her father's port side as they passed at a combined speed of 100 m.p.h.

As they landed John clapped and cheered, and Bart's howl became a joyous barking.

Only Albertina was furious.

'Montagu!' she snapped. 'Whatever do you think you were doing? A fine father you are! Heavens above, you might have killed the child, flying straight at her like that, poor darling! How could you be so stupid and thoughtless, you old fool, you?'

Oh Montagu, Montagu, thought John, now's the time! If ever you're going to stand up to her, do it now. And as though he had spoken this advice out loud, Montagu walked up to his wife and said in even tones, 'Albertina. Hold your tongue.'

A silence followed, broken only by the laughter of a passing woodpecker and a suppressed giggle from Lucky.

Montagu turned to his daughter.

'Right, baby,' he said. 'Off you go.'

'Solo?' said Lucky.

'Yes.'

'But . . .' said Albertina.

'You have clearance,' said Montagu, and Lucky took off again and, gaining height rapidly, treated them to the spectacle of a perfect victory roll. John thought it might be a good idea to disappear. It looked as though a right royal row was about to ensue. But before he had time to call Bart and go, Montagu spoke again.

'Now,' he said, 'after all that excitement and effort, I must confess that I feel a little hungry. Albertina, you may prepare a meal.'

'But . . .' said Albertina.

'NOW.'

'Yes, Monty,' said Albertina Bunsen-Burner.

Six months later, Albertina was preparing a very special meal – for Lucky's first birthday party.

Montagu had been busy for some days catching various delicacies such as sucking-pig, but the main course was to be fish, Lucky's favourite food.

Long before she had learned to fly, she had learned to swim. Or rather, she simply went into the lake for the first time and swam naturally, without any teaching, as did Bart, who had been dog-paddling around with John for some while.

The lake was full of fish, and Lucky soon began to

catch some, liking them so much that she usually breakfasted off them when they all went for their bathe.

But Albertina's plans were more ambitious. Raw fish was all very well, but she planned to fry them for the party. Montagu and John had been roped in to help. Catching enough fish was easy. Montagu simply put his head under in the middle of the lake and blew, causing the water before him to heat up and sending whole shoals floating up to the surface parboiled. Then they rendered down a plump young beast to provide the necessary fat, and John collected a quantity of edible roots in the forest and, with a sword, cut them into long thin slices for frying.

So at last they all sat down to a magnificent spread, the main course of which was fish and chips.

'To think,' said Albertina to her husband. 'Our little Lucky is a whole year old.'

'And growing uglier by the day,' said Montagu. 'Almost as hideous as her mother.'

'Flatterer!' said Albertina coyly.

Quite a change had come over Albertina, John noticed, since that memorable day when the worm, in the shape of Montagu, had turned. She seemed positively to like him being masterful, and if she could not always hold her tongue, she certainly watched her step.

'Let us not forget,' said Montagu, 'that, but for John here, there would have been no Lucky.'

He turned to his daughter.

'You have a lot to thank your brother for, sweetheart,' he said. 'He saved your life, you might say.'

'I know,' said Lucky.

She rubbed her head affectionately against the boy, almost knocking him flat.

'You never know, John,' she said. 'Some day I might save yours.'

12

'We're on Our Own'

One day not long after Lucky's flying test, they were all sitting around in the picnic area. They had lunched well. Montagu and Albertina had had a good morning's hunting, chancing upon a small flock of goats browsing at the forest's edge. The goatherd had run for his life, and all his charges had met their deaths, blasted by the dragons' fiery fusillade.

Now, Montagu and Albertina had eaten two nanny-goats each, and Lucky had polished off a young one.

'A kid for our kid!' joked Montagu.

For John there had been devilled kidneys, and Bart was gnawing a juicy bone.

Montagu burped loudly.

'Very tasty,' he said. 'Makes a nice change.'

Albertina looked thoughtful.

'That gives me an idea,' she said. 'D'you know what else would make a nice change, Monty?'

'No, dear. What?'

'Why, to have a little holiday, to get away for a bit, a long weekend, say. You've been working hard on your flying instruction, Lucky has done so well in her test, and as for me, I shouldn't mind a break from domestic duties – a she-dragon's work is never done.'

'Where do you want to go?'

'How about the seaside? Remember where we went on our honeymoon? The Wash, I think it was called. The air is so bracing and the sea-bathing so healthy. And after a swim, one can just lie on the beach in the sun and do nothing. It would really be good for us, don't you think, Monty?'

Montagu looked doubtful.

'What about the food?' he said. 'You know I prefer good plain home-cooking, Hotlips. Foreign dishes might upset me.'

'Ah, but there will be seals,' said Albertina. 'The Wash is full of seals, don't you remember? Lovely blubbery things, they cook in their own fat. And there are masses of fish, of course. Lucky would have the time of her life, wouldn't you, darling?'

'Oh yes!' cried Lucky. 'Oh Daddy, please can we go to the seaside, please?'

'What about John? And the wolf?' said Montagu.

'Oh, don't worry about us,' said John. 'Anyway, we couldn't come with you – Bart's far too big for me to carry him now and he couldn't balance on any of your backs and I won't leave him here alone. No, you three go off and have a really nice family holiday.'

Now it was Albertina's turn to look worried.

'But will you be all right on your own, John?' she said.

'I shan't be on my own. I'll be perfectly safe with Bart to guard me.'

'We shouldn't be gone long,' said Albertina. 'Two or three days at the most.'

'I'll be as right as rain,' said John.

So the very next day the dragons set off for the seaside. Lucky was highly excited, Albertina was pleased to be leaving household chores behind, and Montagu was now quite looking forward to a spot of seal-hunting.

As John watched and waved goodbye, they formed up in line ahead, Montagu leading, then Lucky, then her mother bringing up the rear, and flew away due east.

'Well, Bart,' said John. 'We're on our own for a while,' and the big black wolf put his ears flat back and waved his bushy tail and licked his master's hand.

It was curious, that first night on their own in the cave. Full of dragons, it had seemed quite a cosy little cave. Now it seemed enormous. And dark. And cold. The dragons' lambent breath, lightly flickering in the gloom, had both lit and warmed the interior, but without them it was chilly, even though summer was not yet done with.

John woke shivering in the small hours, but then he remembered the bearskin. Once dried, it had been rolled up and stored in a crevice in the cave wall, and now he pulled it down, opened it out, fur side up, and lay down on it and wrapped himself in its thick brown warmth. Bart was all right. He had a good black overcoat of his own.

John slept late, and woke to find himself alone. He threw off the bearskin and went outside, to see the wolf lying waiting under the oak.

At sight of his master, he came running, leaping and playing around like a cub, and then running off a little way in a manner that said plainly, 'Come on, lazy-bones! Time for our bathe!'

At the lake, John ran straight in and swam out, enjoying, as always, the shock of the cool water and the thought that it was not only refreshing to be in and to drink, but that it was the easiest possible way to wash both himself and his remnants of ragged clothes.

He floated on his back in the middle, trying to imagine what the dragons would be doing.

Albertina and Montagu might be having a lie-in, he thought, seeing that they're on holiday, but I bet Lucky's gone fishing in the sea. Never in his life having been beyond the boundaries of the forest, he had of course not seen the sea, but Montagu had told him it was like the lake only a million times bigger, and sometimes there were big waves in it, and twice a day it came up the beach and then went down again.

'You can't drink it,' Montagu had said. 'It's too salty.'

What do fish do when they're thirsty, John wondered? He turned over and did a porpoise-dive and swam down deep, imagining himself to be a big fish. When he surfaced again, he saw Bart, whom he had left hunting water-rats among the reeds, paddling towards him at his best speed. He was whining, with anxiety it seemed, and he pawed at John when he reached him, scratching at him, and then turned and looked back towards the shore, growling in his throat.

'What's the matter with you?' John said. 'You look as if you've seen a ghost.'

But then he saw what was sitting on the bank of

the lake, looking at them. It was no ghost but a creature of flesh and blood, and now it was joined by five others like itself.

Ears pricked, red tongues lolling over long white teeth, their bushy tails curled neatly around them, six grey wolves sat in a row and stared at the swimmers.

John's first thought was – am I safe where I am? Or will they, like Bart, be unafraid of water and swim out to attack us?

But the six wolves (one was somewhat bigger than the others, he could see) simply sat silent and waited on the bank, just at the point where he would normally have landed, on his way home.

'We must swim to the far side of the lake then,' he said to Bart, 'and hope that they will lose interest and go away.'

But when he looked back after a couple of dozen strokes, he saw that the wolf-pack's interest in them had not lessened at all. On the contrary, they were already in action, an action that appeared carefully planned.

Five of them had split, two and three, and were racing round the rim of the lake in opposite directions. The sixth, the largest, had stayed where it was. This one, John guessed, was the pack leader, the adult male wolf, and the other five comprised his mate and their four full-grown youngsters. One way or another, it seemed, they were out to prevent John and

Bart from landing, or, if they did, to challenge them.

Already John was shivering. He knew they could not swim around for ever, and the longer he delayed a decision, the more chilled, by fear and fatigue, they would become.

He trod water, holding the paddling Bart by his scruff, until the circling five had run the best part of the way around the lake, and then, with a word to the black wolf, he swam as strongly as he could towards his usual landing-place, straight towards the solitary pack-leader.

He was gambling that it would give way before them and stand aside, so that they could make their escape, to the picnic area, up the field, and into the cave. He did not think that a single wolf would attack a human being, even one his size, and anyway the sight of Bart might deter him.

'Keep close by me, Bart,' he said as his feet struck bottom, 'and don't try anything heroic. He's too big and strong for you to tackle.'

As he had hoped, and to his great relief, the pack-leader stood up and moved easily away to one side, watching them but making no move towards them.

The moment they were out of its sight among the trees, John began to run, as fast as he could, Bart loping beside him. Even as he did so, he heard behind them a single sharp howl, of disappointment, he supposed. It did not occur to him that it was in fact the recall.

At the picnic area he checked long enough to pick up the sword that had belonged to one of the dragons' long-dead knightly victims, the sword which he now used to turn the spit and slice the meat, and then he panted onwards. Up the field, up the hill he went, glancing back over his shoulder, his legs heavy as lead, his chest heaving, until at last they reached the cave mouth.

'We made it, Bart!' gasped John. 'We made it! Let's hope that's the last we'll see of them!'

But the black wolf's only answer was a low growl.

John turned to see him staring back, his hackles raised, his tail held stiffly out behind him.

There, padding quietly up the field in line abreast, as though they had all the time in the world, came the pack.

13

Half a League Onward

John had been quite right – Montagu and Albertina were indeed having a long lie-in on the beach, while Lucky was at sea, fishing.

Fishing was the main occupation of the few folk that lived on that remote eastern edge of the district of Mercia, but no boats had put out that morning. The previous evening some fishermen had been frightened out of their wits by the sudden appearance beside their boat of a 'huge great sea-serpent' (Lucky was by now a good twenty feet long), and others had now seen the two adult dragons on the beach. Those who had doors to their houses bolted and barred them, and a deputation of village elders set off to seek help from the local gentry.

As for the seal colony in that part of the Wash, most were standing out to sea, their round heads sticking up out of the water as they kept watch on the dragons with large anxious eyes. Montagu and Albertina had already celebrated their arrival with a spell of successful hunting.

They were woken now by the incoming tide.

Montagu yawned hotly.

'Sleep well, dearest?' he asked.

'Like a top,' said Albertina. 'It's the sea air. It gives one such an appetite too – I could eat a horse!'

'The problem is,' said Montagu, 'they nearly always have men sitting on them and you said humans were off the menu, remember? For me, that is – I imagine the ban doesn't apply to you?'

'Yes, it does now,' said his wife, and she added, with a touch of her old sharpness, 'I am surprised you should be so insensitive, Montagu. Have you forgotten that our adopted son, thanks to whom our darling daughter was safely born, is a human? Such flesh shall never pass our lips again, is that understood?'

'Yes, dear,' said Montagu, with a touch of his old meekness.

At that moment Lucky came surfing in on a big wave.

'Hello, darling,' said Albertina, and 'Good morning, sweetheart,' said Montagu. 'How was the fishing?'

'Brill!' said Lucky. 'And I caught some brill, what's more, and mackerel, and flounders, and there were some really big sea-bass too – you should have seen the one that got away!' and she spread her paws wide.

'Stop it!' said her mother. 'You're making me hungrier still. Do go and find something for breakfast,

Monty, there's a dear!'

'Oh, very well,' said Montagu, and he taxied along the beach and took off and flew inland, seeking what he might devour.

He had not gone far when he saw below him a company of horsemen. There were a number of knights in full armour, with plumes bobbing on their helmets and pennants fluttering from their lances, while behind them rode their squires carrying such extra armaments as battle-axes and a change of swords.

It was plain that they were not just out to exercise their chargers, and when they caught sight of the dragon high above, loud cries arose, such as, 'Vile Serpent!' 'Loathly Worm!' 'Spawn of the Devil!' and 'Come down and fight!'

Montagu circled above them, listening to this chorus of defiance, and thinking that this part of Merrie England must be woefully short of dragons for these chaps to behave in so inexperienced and rash a manner. Why, he said to himself, they can have no idea of our fire-power, all bunched up together like that, out in the open. One good burst and I could fry the lot! But I suppose I'd better not – Albertina would give me awful stick. At least I must throw a scare into them. They're heading our way, and we don't want our holiday spoiled by a crowd of day-trippers.

Then another thought occurred to him, and he

turned and flew back towards the sea.

Watching him go, scared by their show of force they supposed, the knights and their squires raised a great shout of triumph, and set spurs to their steeds. Each of the knights was determined that it would be he whose trusty lance would pierce the foul heart of the cowardly monster.

Back at the beach, Montagu found his daughter asleep on the sand. Albertina had gone for a dip.

'Lucky,' he said. 'Wake up.'

'What is it, Daddy?'

'You've never yet seen a knight, have you?'

'No, why, is there one coming?'

'Lots of 'em,' said Montagu. 'I thought we might have a bit of fun with them.'

At this point Albertina came up out of the sea.

'What's all this?' she said, and Montagu told her about the approaching enemies.

'We'll scare the iron pants off 'em,' he said.

'No killing, mind,' said Albertina.

'No, no. Listen – here's what we'll do.'

So it was that, a while later, the band of horsemen topped a slight rise, and saw a dragon lying at the far end of a long valley below them. It was a small dragon too, no more than twenty feet in length, not to be compared with the huge monster that had recently overflown them, and to cap it all, it seemed to be fast asleep.

Everyone suddenly felt much braver. Each knight settled himself in his saddle, his lance couched, his reins firmly gripped in one mailed fist, and urged his charger into line upon the crest.

Then, with a cry of, 'Forward the Knight Brigade!' they all rode down into the valley.

First trotting, then cantering, and then at full gallop they sped along its bed, half a league onward, each man bringing his lance down to the horizontal as they neared the small sleeping dragon, when suddenly it leaped to its feet and let out a jet of flame. At the same instant two other enormous dragons suddenly appeared on either flank of the charging

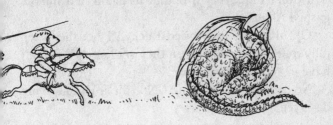

cavalry, and the air before them became a holocaust of fire as they rode, it seemed, into the mouth of hell.

Dragon to right of them, dragon to left of them, dragon in front of them volleyed and thundered, and in total panic the bold knights of Mercia turned as one man, and hightailed it back up the valley of death as fast as they could caper.

Montagu and Albertina and Lucky switched off and lay about shaking with laughter.

'Oh dear, oh dear!' snorted Montagu. 'Pity they had their visors down – I'd have loved to see the expressions on their faces!'

'I don't think they'll bother us again in a hurry!' gasped Albertina.

'Oh, that was fun!' cried Lucky. 'I bet they keep jolly quiet about that when they get home! We don't have to go home yet, do we?'

'No, no,' said Albertina. 'Not for a couple more days yet.'

'The weather's too good to miss,' said Montagu. 'Now then, Hotlips, you and I have had no breakfast yet. Let's go and get some seafood.'

As they were flying back to the beach, Lucky said to her parents, 'John will be all right, won't he?'

'Oh yes,' they said.

14

'Up and at 'Em!'

As the wolf-pack came steadily and silently up the field, John suddenly realized with a chill of horror that the cave was not the place of safety it had seemed as he was running towards it. Always before it had been a refuge because of the presence of Montagu or Albertina, but now it was just a cave with a very large, dragon-sized entrance, roomy enough for a hundred wolves to come pouring through it.

How was he to keep these six out?

One thing was plain – for him and Bart to retreat into the interior of the cave would be suicidal. They would be trapped, and might be rushed at any moment. There was no alternative for them but to stay in the cave's mouth, where they could keep watch on the pack, at least in daylight.

Maybe they would not attack. Maybe they were just curious. Maybe they could be scared away.

He swung the sword round his head, with great difficulty, for it was heavy, and yelled, 'Aaaaaargh! Go away or I'll cut your heads off!'

At the sound of his voice the pack stopped, a mere ten yards away now, and sat down, the leader a little in advance of the rest.

John had been right in thinking that wolves will not usually attack humans, but wrong in thinking that they were interested in him. It was Bart they were after.

It was the natural reaction of wild animals to one of their own kind who behaves in a different, unnatural manner. What was this black wolf doing following a human like a dog? He was an outcast, they felt angrily, who acted oddly and smelled strange, and if the boy had not been there, they would have gone in and killed him now.

As it was, they lay down, and waited for the night.

John and Bart waited too, for there was little else they could do. There was nothing to eat or drink either, though both were hungry and thirsty.

What wouldn't I give to see the dragons come flying home, thought John. Why, Lucky alone would soon see this lot off. But they may be away for another day or more yet. And it will be dark before long, and chilly out here too. I shall need the bearskin.

He put a hand on top of Bart's head and pressed. Then, very slowly, he began to back into the cave. Before he had gone very far, the pack leader stood up, his eyes fixed upon the black wolf alone now in the cave mouth, and he moved a couple of paces nearer. Then he withdrew again as John came hastily back to stand beside Bart. The bearskin would have to wait till after dark.

But after dark he did not dare try again, for though he could now see little of the wolves, they, he knew, could see him clearly. So he remained upright, leaning upon his sword, his own wolf at his side.

Empty-bellied, shivering with cold now, and tired out with the strain of waiting, John suddenly felt he could not stand up a moment longer. He sat down on the ground, and, as the hunter's moon rose to light the scene, his head fell forward on his chest and his eyes closed.

Next moment he was not only wide awake but flat on his back as a heavy body knocked him flying. With a snarl of hatred, the grey leader had hurled himself at the black renegade.

John never forgot the scene that met his eyes as he scrambled to his feet again, fumbling for the fallen sword.

There in the yellow moonlight Bart and the pack-leader fought in single combat, not in the close-quarter grappling of a dog-fight, but in true wolf fashion, leaping in and out again, slashing at one another in passing, light on their feet as cats. In the background the other five wolves padded to and fro, whining.

John could only watch helplessly as the battle raged, not daring to intervene for fear of striking Bart by mistake with the heavy sword.

The grey was the heavier and the stronger, but

Bart was younger and quicker on his feet, and, most importantly, he was fighting for his life and, as he thought, for the life of his master. He was superbly fit too, thanks to the good feeding he always received at the dragons' table, and that black coat was thick enough to withstand the ripping attacks of the older animal.

The leader was the first to tire, and in the next exchange he was just too slow to avoid Bart's counter-stroke, which tore one of his ears to ribbons. As he hesitated, shaking his head, John darted in with the sword and jabbed at him with the point of it, so that he sprang away with a yowl, and slunk back to rejoin the pack.

Now the rest will come, thought John, but they did not.

Neither did they go, and dawn broke to find them all still lying before the cave mouth while the she-wolf licked at her mate's ruined ear. Now and then she broke off to turn her head and stare at Bart, growling in her throat. Sooner or later, she was plainly saying, we will kill you.

'Sooner or later,' said John, 'we are going to have to take them on, Bart, no matter what the odds. They'll come for us in a body tonight – that's for sure. If we don't first starve to death or die of thirst. We must charge straight at them, there's no other way. At least we'll take one or two of them with us, if we have to go down fighting.'

He stroked the black head, and took a firm grip on his sword.

'Now then, Bart,' he said. 'Up and at 'em!'

For a moment, as they ran forward, it looked as though escape was on the cards, for the pack parted before them and let them through. But this, they soon found, was with a purpose, for the six wolves swung after them, intent upon attack from the rear. A favourite tactic of the hunting wolf is to hamstring its fleeing prey – to lame it by biting through the great tendon at the back of the leg, thus rendering it powerless – and as they ran down the field, this is what first one and then another of the pack tried to do. In the wild excitement of the chase any fear of man was lost, for now the law of the mob ruled, and soon John was tripped as a wolf tried for a hold on his leg and missed. He fell – at the exact spot, had he known it, where Bart's mother had fallen, never to rise again – and as he went down, encumbered with the heavy sword, he hit his head on something hard that was buried in the grass, and knocked himself out.

Bravely Bart straddled his master's prone body, snarling defiance as the pack poured over them.

Fifty miles (as the dragon flies) to the east, and just over an hour earlier, Lucky woke with a start as the first daylight began to creep across the wrinkled surface of the sea.

Animals of many kinds need to and do trust their

instincts in a way that a human being never would, and something told Lucky, beyond any doubt, that John and Bart were in deep trouble.

She considered waking Montagu and Albertina and telling them of her fears, but then she said to herself, no, I'm a big girl now, I can handle this on my own. And, anyway, she did not want to disturb her parents – they looked so peaceful and happy as they lay side by side on the beach. There were silly grins on their hideous sleeping faces, as if they were still on that honeymoon of fifty years ago, though now each carried a good few extra hundredweights of middle-aged spread.

I'd better leave them a message though, thought Lucky, and, using her tail as a marker, she drew in the sand a large arrow, pointing due west. Then she went quietly to the far end of the beach and took off.

Dragons, like many flying creatures such as pigeons or swallows, have a very accurate sense of direction, a kind of built-in compass that takes them unerringly to their destination. So in just over fifty minutes Lucky saw the fringes of the great forest beneath her and flew lower, looking for the line of rocky cliffs in which was the dragons' cave. Soon she spotted the lake and knew she was dead on course.

But now what was that fearful noise of furious growling and yowling and snarling, what was that mêlée of struggling shapes, in the home field, not far from the oak tree? Wolves! At a kill!

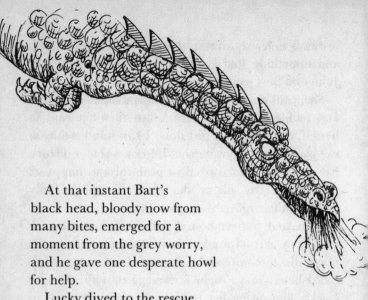

At that instant Bart's
black head, bloody now from
many bites, emerged for a
moment from the grey worry,
and he gave one desperate howl
for help.

Lucky dived to the rescue.

For John the whole of this dreadful drama was a merciful blank, from the moment he fell until he came to his senses once more, under the impression that he was being washed with a huge, hot, wet flannel.

In fact, he was being licked by Lucky's large tongue, and now as he sat up, he could see Bart lying close by, also licking at the wounds that the pack had inflicted on his black hide.

'Speak to me, little brother! Speak to me!' cried Lucky anxiously. 'Have they hurt you? Are you all right?'

John examined himself gingerly. There was a lump the size of a hen's egg on his forehead, while his ragged remnants of clothing were now so torn as to be more holes than material, but, thanks to Bart's protection, he did not seem to have been bitten, though he was scratched and bruised all over.

'Zounds!' he said. 'I'm sore. But look at my Bart! Poor boy, they've used you cruelly!'

'He's all right,' said Lucky. 'No bones broken, and those cuts will soon heal. But I wasn't a moment too soon. They'd have finished him before long, and you after.'

'What's become of them?' said John.

'They ran off when I landed,' said Lucky. 'I couldn't blast them here for fear of frying Bart – at that point I couldn't see you under the scrimmage, I didn't even know you were there. I let them go and then I followed.'

'But they may come back!'

'No,' said Lucky. 'They won't come back. Unless you believe in ghosts.'

'Oh,' said John. 'You said you might save my life one day, remember?'

'Think nothing of it, little brother,' said Lucky. 'One good turn deserves another. Let's have a good look at you now. My, my, you've had a bump on the head!'

'I must have hit it on something when I fell,' John said.

Lucky searched about in the long grass and turned up something with her snout.

'I should think it was this,' she said. 'Of all things, an old skull.'

She nosed at it.

'Funny,' she said. 'It looks like a wolf's.'

15

A Clothes-hunt

Albertina Bunsen-Burner woke from a good night's sleep with a feeling of pleasant anticipation. The weather, she could see, remained fine, and there was still one more day of the seaside holiday to enjoy. A swim before breakfast was an attractive idea, she thought, and as Montagu was still fast asleep, she turned to ask her daughter if she fancied a dip.

But Lucky was not there.

Albertina looked out to sea, but there was no sign of her, either there or anywhere along the beach.

'Montagu!' she said sharply to her husband.

'Wassup?' said Montagu drowsily.

'Lucky's not here.'

'Mussbe somewhere else then.'

'But where? Where would she go? Why would she go? Where has she gone?'

'Dunno,' said Montagu.

He gave an enormous yawn and settled back comfortably.

'Shouldn't worry if I were you,' he said. 'She's a big girl now, you know.'

'You are *not* me,' said Albertina, 'and I *am* worried. You seem to forget that our only child is very young and, contrary to your idea of her size, very small. Kindly get up immediately and help me search for her, d'you hear?'

'Oh, very well, dear,' said Montagu, and he heaved himself to his feet as Albertina lumbered off along the beach.

'Lucky! Lucky!' she bellowed as she went. 'Where are you, darling? Come to Mummy,' while the gulls screamed around her and rows of anxious seals' heads bobbed up out in the waters of the Wash.

Montagu set off in the opposite direction, but he had not gone far before he came upon the pictorial message that Lucky had drawn in the sand. He studied it with interest. It looks like an arrow, he thought.

He was still studying it when Albertina returned from her fruitless search.

'See this?' he said. 'Lucky must have drawn it. It looks like an arrow.'

'It *is* an arrow,' said Albertina.

'Good, isn't it?' said Montagu. 'I didn't think she could draw as well as that. I didn't know she was so clever.'

'And she didn't know you were so stupid,' said his wife acidly. 'Do you not see the point of it?'

Montagu looked at the point of the arrow.

'Yes,' he said.

'Well then? What does it mean?'

Montagu thought for a while. Then he shook his head.

'I give up,' he said.

'It is pointing west,' said Albertina slowly between her teeth. 'It is pointing towards home. Lucky has flown home.'

'Oh,' said Montagu.

'Why?' he said.

At this Albertina lost her temper.

'How do I know?' she shouted. 'That's what I'm going to find out. As for you, you might just as well stay here. You're too brainless to be of any use!' and she flew away inland at her best speed.

How hideous the old girl looks when she's angry, thought Montagu fondly. Ah well, I suppose I'd better follow.

Perhaps Lucky was homesick, he thought as he flapped along. After all, she's never been away before. And, come to think of it, I shall be jolly glad to see the old place again. Holidays are all very well, but there's nowhere quite like your own pad. And I'm getting a bit sick of blubbery seal and salty fish – the roast beef of Olde England, that's what I fancy right now. At that precise moment he saw below him a herd of cattle, and he dived down and slew the fattest beast.

Carrying this heavy burden home reduced his air speed, so that by the time he touched down outside the cave, Lucky and John had told Albertina everything that had happened, and Montagu had to be told all over again.

'You did a grand job by the sound of it, sweetheart,' he said proudly to his daughter. Chip off the old block, he was about to say, but then he thought that a more tactful remark might put him back in his wife's good books.

'Just like your mother, you are, Lucky,' he said. 'Not only perfectly revolting to look at, but brave and resourceful and quick-thinking and . . .'

'Yes, yes, Monty, that's enough,' said Albertina, but she did not sound displeased. 'Lucky has done very well, but just look at our boy. Poor John is a mass of bruises.'

'Got just the thing for that,' said Montagu. 'Nothing like a good big raw beefsteak to slap on a bruise, and I dare say Bart will find a good use for it afterwards.'

'But just look at John's clothes,' said Albertina. 'They're only hanging together by threads.'

'Never bothered with clothes myself,' said Montagu.

'That's because you've got a good thick skin, Daddy,' said Lucky.

'And central heating,' said John. 'If I was to go about the forest with no clothes on, I'd be ripped and scratched to bits by all the briars and brambles, and I'd freeze to death in winter.'

'Which will be here before long,' said Albertina. 'We must do something about it before then.'

'I'll be all right at nights,' John said, 'in the bearskin. I suppose the only thing to do is to try and make myself some clothes from the skins of other animals that you kill. But I really need the kind of things that humans wear.'

'Well, that's easy,' said Lucky. 'We'll catch a human about your size and make him take his clothes off.'

'Wait a minute,' said Albertina. 'Don't forget John's a growing boy. Better to get a couple of sizes too big.'

'And you might as well catch several humans while you're about it,' said Montagu. 'That way you'll have a choice, and a change of clothing too. And as for the chaps themselves, well, we could always make use of them, couldn't we, Hotlips?'

'No,' said Albertina firmly. 'And another thing, Monty – you are not going on this expedition, so just stop licking your lips. Whatever must John think of you?'

'There's no need for either of you to come,' said Lucky quickly. 'John and I will manage quite nicely on our own.'

So after a while, during which the boy's bruises paled and the wolf's wounds healed and the dragon family settled back happily into their workaday routine, Lucky and John set off on a clotheshunt.

John had given the matter a good deal of thought and had realized two things. First, their chances of seeing and catching many people in the forest were slim. They would have to visit a town. Second, that town had better not be too near. Like the fox who avoids the farmyard close to his earth and is careful to take his chickens from a distant hen-run, John decided that they must hunt a good long way from home.

That meant air travel, and that in its turn meant that Bart must stay behind. John explained this to the black wolf, feeling confident that the animal understood and that he would now be quite safe in the charge of Montagu and Albertina.

It crossed his mind that any one of the saddles

between Lucky's dorsal fins might not be big enough for him, and indeed it was a bit of a tight fit, but all the safer for that, and so one fine morning away they went.

High above the great forest they flew, so high that at last they could see below them the whole vast expanse of it, the green of its millions of trees turning now to the gold and russet shades of autumn. Then they turned north and flew on until finally they came to a countryside of quite a different sort, of bare, rolling, rocky uplands split by deep dales.

It was not long before they saw in one of these dales a small town.

As they lost altitude, they could see that their luck was in – that Lucky was living up to her name – for not only was it a market town, but they had chanced upon it on market day. The square in its centre was filled with booths and stalls and livestock and people.

No sooner was the dragon sighted than utter confusion reigned. Cattle and sheep and pigs and horses stampeded in all directions, and people rushed for the shelter of nearby houses or threw themselves down behind their stalls or under the beds of their wagons.

A wild chorus of screams and yells of fear greeted Lucky's landing in the now empty centre of the market square, and then all fell suddenly silent at the sight that met their astonished eyes.

To see a dragon was bad enough, but to see a dragon ridden by a boy!

'Mercy! Mercy!' cried those nearest, falling upon their knees. 'Spare our lives, young master!' but not all, John's sharp eyes noticed, were as cowed. There were no knights among this rustic throng, but there was a number of freemen privileged to carry arms to defend their flocks and herds against wild beasts, and several of them were fitting arrows to their bows.

'Let but one man take aim at me,' shouted John, standing upright upon Lucky's pale-green back, 'and my dragon shall burn you all and your town to ashes! Throw down your weapons, all that carry them!'

When this had been done, he climbed down and walked towards a boy of about his own height.

'You there,' he said. 'How old are you?'

'N-nigh on t-ten years of age, your honour,' squeaked the boy.

Same as me, thought John.

'Take off your jerkin,' he said, 'and give it to me.'

Only now, when John tried the jerkin on and found it much too tight across the shoulders, did he realize how big and strong he had grown. Why, there were men among the crowd not much bigger than him. He remembered the advice that Albertina and Montagu had given him, and decided it would be best to take a selection of everything. He pointed

136

at a knot of a dozen men and youths, huddled in a corner of the square.

'You there!' he said. 'Step forward!'

As they hesitated, Lucky blew a casual jet of flame over their heads, and then they hastily obeyed.

'Now,' said John, 'take your clothes off.'

Another jet of fire removed any thoughts the twelve might have had of disobeying this order, and in a moment they stood in their underwear, their jerkins and doublets and tunics and shirts and breeches and boots piled before them.

From all around the square came sniggers and giggles as men and women momentarily forgot their terror at the sight of their fellows in a state of undress. What would the boy do next?

'What do I do next?' said John in Lucky's ear. 'I shall need warm underclothing once winter sets in, but I don't like to leave these poor devils naked. Anyway, I don't much fancy theirs – they look none too clean.'

'There's a stall yonder that sells the things, see?' said Lucky, and, sure enough, there, laid out upon a bench, was a pile of thick combinations woven from the warm wool of the upland sheep.

Now it was simply a matter of packaging up John's ill-gotten goods.

Under his orders, the twelve shivering unfortunates laid out a tarpaulin and upon it they put all their discarded apparel and the woollen underclothes. Then its corners were folded in and tied into a huge bundle, which Lucky took in her teeth. Lastly, John remounted.

'I thank you, goodmen all,' he said. 'I shall not forget you.'

Nor did they forget him.

Even now, I am told, many hundreds of years later, folk in that little market town in the dales still tell their children the story of the coming of the dragon boy.

16

The Forest Fire

The very next day, as though to celebrate the arrival of John's new wardrobe, a strong easterly wind began the work of stripping the forest trees of their summer clothing. Leaves of every colour and shape blew wildly everywhere, and the red squirrels set about building up their stores of hazelnuts and beech-mast against the coming of winter.

The dragons, of course, did not feel the cold, and nor did Bart in his thick black coat,

but John was thankful to have made a heap of his old rags for Lucky to incinerate and to be more warmly dressed than he had ever been in his life.

Next to his skin he wore a set of the woollen combinations, snug-fitting to neck and wrist and ankle, and over this a shirt and a doublet on his upper half and stout breeches on his lower. Finally he had selected from all the footwear on offer a knee-length pair of stout cowhide boots, and, to top it all, a round hat of squirrel fur, the bushy tail hanging down his back.

'Doesn't he look smart!' said Lucky to her parents.

'Quite the man,' said Montagu.

Albertina cast a maternal eye over her adopted child.

'Stand up straight,' she said. 'Now turn round. Yes. Very nice. Do the boots fit?'

'They're a bit big,' said John, 'but I've got two pairs of woollen socks on.'

He stamped his feet appreciatively.

'These boots were made for walking,' he said. 'Come, Bart, let's stretch our legs.'

The three dragons watched as boy and beast strode away down the field, past the oak, past the wolf-skull in the grass, past the flat outcrop of rock in the picnic area, until they disappeared into the forest.

'My, how he's grown!' said Albertina.

'Pity he's so handsome,' said Montagu, 'but that's not his fault. Not everyone can be as ugly as our little girl.'

'Mummy?' said the little girl, who by now had grown in length by another six feet.

'Yes, darling?'

'Were you disappointed that I wasn't a boy?'

'No, darling, no! I was thrilled to bits to have a daughter and so was your father, weren't you, Monty?'

'Happiest day of my life,' said Montagu.

'So far,' he added.

'Why?' said Lucky. 'Is there going to be a happier one?'

She turned to her mother.

'Mummy!' she said. 'Is there something you haven't told me? You're not . . . . eggnant, are you?'

'No, no,' said Albertina. 'Mummy's too old now to have any more babies.'

'What did you mean then, Daddy,' said Lucky, 'when you said "Happiest day so far"?'

'I was thinking of the day when you hatch out eggs of your own, sweetheart,' said Montagu. 'We Bunsen-Burners marry young as a rule. I can't wait to be a grandfather!'

'Fat chance I've got of marrying!' said Lucky. 'Why, the only other dragon I've set eyes on so far is that old Examiner and he's about a hundred and fifty!' and she flew off in a tizzy.

'The child is right,' said Albertina. 'There seems to be a great shortage of eligible young dragons these days. It was not so when you were courting me, Monty, remember? You had quite a few rivals.'

'Rivals?' said Montagu. 'I'd hardly call them that. Callow youths as I recall, the Fryer lad, young Grillem, and that boy who flew across from Galway – what was his name now, Blazer, that's it. I soon saw them off.'

'You did, Monty, you did. But then you were already full-grown of course. You swept me off my feet!'

Shouldn't like to try it now, thought Montagu.

'Coming back to Lucky,' went on Albertina. 'Maybe we should be making plans for her now. If dragons are becoming as scarce as it would seem, we had better look around – in distant regions perhaps – for some young fellow of good family whose parents would approve such a match.'

'An arranged marriage, do you mean?' said Montagu.

A romantic at heart, he did not like the idea of his beloved Lucky being paired off with some young whipper-snapper. On the other hand, he thought, half a loaf is better than no bread, and it would be terrible if she were left on the shelf, he did so want grandchildren.

With her she-dragon's intuition, Albertina guessed what her husband was thinking, and she settled the matter cleverly.

'Yes,' she said, 'an arranged marriage. But only if *you* approve the idea, Monty dearest. I would not dream of proceeding without your consent.'

Thus it was that shortly afterwards Lucky's mother and father set off, one to the west, one to the south, in search of a suitable future son-in-law.

Lucky meanwhile had flown some little way – to the east, as it happened – in a childish sulk. I'll get married when I want to and not before, she said to herself. It's none of their business. Grown-ups!

As she flew across the lake, she considered splashing down and having a swim and a good meal of fish, but then dismissed the idea just because it would have been a nice thing to do and she was in the mood to be nasty to herself as well as to anyone she met.

Soon she sighted John and Bart walking in the same direction. John waved at her, but sulky Lucky took no notice.

She flew on until by chance she spotted a number of rabbits in an open patch of scrub, sitting outside their holes or grazing or hopping about, and decided to vent her bad temper upon them. She dived low, shooting out a long jet of flame.

In fact, the rabbits were too quick for her, popping down their burrows before the jet could strike them, but it was to do far, far more damage than thoughtless Lucky could have imagined.

It had been a long arid summer, and almost everything in the forest was tinder-dry, nothing more so than the gorse and bracken that covered the area where the rabbits had dug their homes in the sandy soil.

Lucky flew on, unaware of the result of her hot temper.

Within minutes the whole patch of scrub was ablaze, and a line of flames, fanned by the strong east wind and growing higher and longer as it went, moved steadily across the open ground and into the bordering trees.

If it had not been for the wind, the flames might perhaps have gone no further, for there was still plenty of sap in the leaves. But as it was, first one and then another great tree caught alight as the blaze spread and grew into an enormous bank of fire.

The first that John knew of it was the sight of many birds and small beasts on the move, flying or running or hopping or wriggling towards and past him. Then he smelled smoke. Then he heard the crackle and dull roar of the still distant fire, noises that grew louder by the minute, until at last he could see it, a red-and-orange wall of flame as high as a house, coming straight towards him and Bart.

John turned and began to run, the wolf at his heels.

At first, though he was frightened, he did not

144

appreciate the danger. The lake, after all, was not much more than half a mile back, and even in his clumsy new boots he could surely reach the safety of it easily. But he had not bargained with the strength of that cold easterly gale nor with the dryness of the undergrowth of fern and bracken and briar.

He was going as fast as a boy can go.

The forest fire was moving now with the speed of a galloping horse.

For the second time in his life John was running for it, running desperately now, glancing wildly back over his shoulder as the fire gained on him. Twice he tripped and fell while Bart whined anxiously at him to get up again, and now the roar of the flames was very loud.

At last, just as he felt that his lungs must burst and that he simply could not put one heavy-booted foot in front of the other any more, he broke through a screen of bushes and there before them was the lake, into which Bart dashed.

With one last desperate effort, even as a tongue of fire licked out and singed the squirrel tail that hung down his back, John stumbled forward and fell head-long into the welcoming water.

17

A Very Long Day

Killing a few bunnies (as she thought) had taken the edge off Lucky's bad mood, and she flew on now in a better frame of mind. At first she had been flying aimlessly, but now, recognizing certain landmarks, she realized that she was, in fact, on the holiday route, heading straight for the seaside.

'I will have that bathe after all,' she said, 'and do a bit of fishing too. Won't Mummy and Daddy be surprised when I tell them where I've been!'

It was she, though, who was to be surprised before long when she reached the coast and prepared to land on the beach where they had spent their holiday. There, stretched out on the sands fast asleep, was another dragon!

Lucky hovered overhead, staring angrily down. What right had this creature to lie about on *her* family's beach?

The intruder, she could see, was young, about her own size or a little larger, and of what she had to admit was an engagingly unattractive colour, a kind of a shade of buff with pinkish undertones. But that didn't entitle him or her to trespass.

Lucky landed.

'Hey, you!' she said loudly.

The intruder woke with a start.

'What d'you think you're doing?' said Lucky.

'I *was* sleeping.'

'Well, now you're awake, you can buzz off. This is a private beach. Who are you anyway?'

'My name is Gerald.'

Gerald, thought Lucky – a boy, eh? Despite her annoyance, she felt rather glad. At close quarters the young dragon, she was relieved to see, was not at all

good-looking. Indeed he was distinctly homely, not to say as plain as a pikestaff.

'Gerald who?' she said.

'Fire-Drake.'

'Well, Mr Gerald Fire-Drake,' said Lucky. 'What are you doing on my family's bathing-beach?'

'I'm awfully sorry,' said Gerald. 'Miss . . . er?'

'Bunsen-Burner.'

'I'm awfully sorry, Miss Bunsen-Burner. I hadn't realized it was private.'

'Well, you do now.'

'Yes,' said Gerald.

He yawned hugely.

'I beg your pardon,' he said, 'but I'm absolutely whacked. Fact is, I've run away from home, flown away, I should say. Had a blazing row with Father and he told me to clear out, so I did. It's been a very long flight, you see – we've got a place up in Scotland.'

This speech aroused a fellow-feeling in Lucky.

'Oh, all right,' she said. 'You get some sleep,' and she turned away.

'Where are you going?' said Gerald.

'Fishing.'

'You'll come back, won't you?'

'I might.'

'Please do. By the way, I don't know your first name.'

'Lucky.'

'Lucky!' said Gerald Fire-Drake as he watched her paddling out to sea. 'What a simply hideous name!' and, smiling happily, he lay down again and went back to sleep.

Into Lucky's head, as she swam about in the still, warm waters of the Wash, came an idea.

Her new friend (for thus she already thought of him) had run away from his home. She would invite him to hers! Mummy and Daddy wouldn't mind putting him up for a while. And John would like another chap to chat to. And . . . she broke off her chain of thought to catch a big fish and swallow it . . . And, she said to herself with a giggle, I must admit that Gerald is, well, awfully ugly!

While these thoughts struck Lucky, her father and mother were not enjoying such good fortune.

Montagu, who had flown in a southerly direction, did indeed come across a family of dragons in Wessex named Charmouth, and was getting on with the parents like a house on fire (as dragons usually do). He did not reveal the nature of his mission, thinking it wiser first to enjoy the hospitality he was offered. But when the meal (a fine fat bullock) was finished and he had complimented his hostess, he asked her, somewhat hesitantly for he could see none, if she had children.

'Oh yah!' said Mrs Charmouth. 'Masses!'

Great, thought Montagu!

'They're not at home?' he said.

'Gorn huntin'.'

'Frightfully keen, doncherknow,' said Mr Charmouth. 'Could fly before they could walk. Blooded before they were a couple of months old, all of 'em. Not many blank days when our youngsters are out, ask anybody round here. And go – can they go! Yoicks! Tally-ho! What?'

'Jolly good,' said Montagu. 'How many have you, in fact?'

'Seven,' said Mrs Charmouth.

Seven, thought Montagu, there's sure to be a young fellow to suit Lucky among that lot!

'You got sprogs of your own?' asked Mr Charmouth.

'Just the one girl,' said Montagu. 'Matter of fact, my wife and I are very keen to see her married off. Are any of yours of marriageable age?'

'Oh yah!' said Mrs Charmouth. 'Longin' to get them settled down. Be glad when they're all gorn. No joke, y'know, havin' seven gels.'

Albertina had flown into Wales, the land, had she known it, of that great British chieftain of long ago, Uther Pendragon. Never before had she ventured so far west, and soon she found herself flying over mountains.

Indeed, the first dragon she saw was sitting on a mountain. Albertina landed beside it.

Like all Welsh dragons, it was smaller than average and of a bright red colour, and before Albertina could open her mouth, it began to jabber at her in a foreign language of which she could not understand a word, so she flew on again.

With the next red dragon she met on the next mountain she had better luck.

'Do you speak English?' was her first question.

'Bilingual I am, see,' was the reply.

'Ah,' said Albertina. She was not sure what the

first word meant. But at least I can understand this one, she thought.

'I am Mrs Bunsen-Burner,' she said.

'Fancy!' said the red dragon. 'There's nice.'

What a strange accent, thought Albertina, and what a scruffy little individual. There must be a better class of dragon than this in Wales.

'I should be grateful,' she said in a patronizing tone, 'if you would help me, my good fellow.'

'I doubt it,' said the red dragon. 'To begin with, I am not your good fellow, look you, and secondly, I know what you're looking for.'

'You do?'

'Yes, indeed to goodness – a second home, that's what you're after. Just because you can afford a holiday cave, a Welsh family has to do without. You'd better be careful, Mrs Whatsit, unless you want to be burned out.'

'I don't know what on earth you are talking about,' said Albertina stiffly. 'I am, in fact, looking for a suitable husband for my young daughter. I don't imagine you are acquainted with any of the old-established families in this area?'

Highly unlikely, she thought. I mean, nobody could call me a snob, but this fellow seems awfully common, though no doubt he would give his eye-teeth for one of his own sons to have the chance of marrying my Lucky.

She was mistaken.

'What colour is your daughter, may I ask?' said the Welsh dragon.

'Green,' said Albertina loftily.

'Green?' said the Welsh dragon on a note of horror.

'Listen here,' he said, 'and listen carefully. First, I am the head of one of the oldest families in Wales. Second, though I have three sons, I would not dream of allowing our Gwyn, our Owen or our Llewellyn even to consider an alliance with your daughter. We do not approve of mixed marriages in our country, look you. And third, don't ever show your pretty English face on my mountain again. Now beat it, before I whistle up the boys.'

*

Albertina flew home in the foulest of tempers. When she arrived that evening, tired and hungry for, unlike her husband, she had had nothing to eat, she found John dressed in quite different clothes from those he had been wearing that morning. His wet ones were spread across some bushes, and Montagu was drying them with careful blasts of hot air.

'What is going on?' said Albertina.

'There was a forest fire,' John said. 'Bart and I only just escaped. We stood in the lake up to our necks until it had passed.'

'What caused it?' said Albertina. 'Montagu, did you . . . ?'

'No, no, my dear,' said Montagu. 'I was down in Wessex. I've only just returned.'

'Did you have any luck?'

'Afraid not. Found a very decent sort of family, but they had nothing but daughters. How about you, Hotlips? How did you get on? Did you find anyone suitable in Wales?'

'No,' said Albertina shortly. She had no intention, now or ever, of revealing how she had been humiliated.

'What were you both looking for?' asked John.

'A possible future husband for your sister,' said Albertina.

'She's very young,' said John.

'It would simply be an arrangement, you know,' said Montagu. 'An understanding.'

'A long engagement, you mean?'

'Yes. To someone we consider suitable.'

'She might not like him,' said John.

'Liking doesn't enter into it,' said Albertina. 'Lucky will marry whom we wish. Where is she, by the way? Not back yet? It is growing dark.'

In fact, it was quite dark by the time Lucky and Gerald reached the eastern edge of the forest, so that they could not see the black swathe that the fire had cut through it.

They had spent a long, happy day doing the things all children like to do at the seaside – bathing, picnicking and playing games on the sands, and each had privately decided the other was very nice.

As they neared the cave, flying side by side, Lucky said, 'I think it might be best if I go in first and prepare Mummy and Daddy. Would you mind landing by that oak tree and staying there until I give you a shout?'

John was outside collecting his dry clothes from the bushes when he saw not one, but two young dragons land, and he guessed immediately what had happened. He was pretty sure in his own mind that it was Lucky who had started the forest fire, and he fully intended to tackle her about the thoughtlessness that had almost cost him and Bart their lives. But not tonight, he thought, not now, when she is just about to introduce a boyfriend and when Albertina is in a filthy mood anyway.

'Oh, hello, John,' said Lucky. 'Sorry about this morning.'

'How do you mean?' said John.

'When you waved at me. I rather cut you dead.'

Dead was nearly the word, thought John.

'I was feeling grumpy,' said Lucky. 'Did you have a nice walk?'

'Oh yes,' said John. 'More of a run really.'

He followed her into the cave.

'Hello, sweetheart!' cried Montagu. 'There you are at last. We were getting worried.'

'Worried and angry,' said Albertina. 'Whatever have you been doing, my girl?'

'I've been at the seaside.'

'At the seaside?'

'Yes. I met a boy there.'

'A boy?' said Albertina. 'Do you mean a dragon boy, like John, or a boy dragon?'

'A boy dragon,' said Lucky. 'He's nice. We had fun, playing games on the beach.'

Albertina and Montagu looked at one another.

'And where is he now?' said Albertina.

'He's outside,' said Lucky. 'I brought him back with me. He's had a row with his people, you see, and flown away from home, and I thought maybe he could stay with us for a bit. Would that be all right?'

Albertina did not answer,
but Montagu said, 'Of course,
sweetheart!' so Lucky went
to the mouth of the cave
and called, 'Gerald!'
  'Gerald?' said Albertina
on a rising note, and then
shortly he appeared.

'Gerald,' said Lucky, 'come and meet my mother and my father and my brother. Mummy, Daddy, John – this is Gerald Fire-Drake.'

'How do you do, Mrs Bunsen-Burner? How do you do, sir? Hello, John,' said Gerald.

'Fire-Drake?' said Montagu. 'I went to the dragon school with a Fire-Drake, came from an old Scottish family. Especially fine flyer, I remember, flew rings round the rest of us chaps.'

'That's my father, sir,' said Gerald.

Albertina was by now looking a good deal less disapproving, and Gerald's next remark was particularly well chosen.

'What a simply hideous home you have, Mrs Bunsen-Burner,' he said. 'I don't think I've ever seen such an unattractive cave.'

'Oh!' said Albertina. 'How kind of you to say so!'

'But I mustn't trespass further on your hospitality,' said Gerald. 'I'll find somewhere to doss down outside.'

'Nonsense, my boy!' said Montagu. 'There's a spare grotto at the back of the cave that you're most welcome to. You must both be tired after such a long day.'

'Yes,' said Lucky, yawning. 'It's all right for you and Mummy and John – I don't suppose you've done anything much. But for Gerald and me it's been a very long day.'

18

'You Should Have Seen It!'

The following morning John and Lucky and Gerald stood beside the lake.

Montagu had gone hunting, and Albertina, spurred on by Gerald's complimentary remarks, was busy with housework. Bart lay under the oak tree, for John had thought it best not to take him with them. The dragons' fireproof feet and his own stout boots would be protection enough, but Bart's pads, he thought, might be burned by the still hot forest floor.

In fact, John could now see, the fire could well have been much worse. Thanks to the speed with which the wind had carried it, it had run straight at the lake without spreading sideways and been brought to a halt by the body of water and the thick reed-beds which damped its efforts to encircle the lake. Only a few hundred acres out of the vast expanse of the greenwood had actually burned down, but that in itself was an awful sight.

Great numbers of fine trees, chestnut and beech and oak, some several centuries old, were now but blackened skeletons, some fallen, some still forlornly standing, their charred trunks stripped of branches and leaves. The lesser growth, of bushes and saplings, was all gone, and everywhere, as the three could now see when they walked on, there were pathetic little scorched corpses, of bird or beast or reptile that had been too slow or too young or too panic-stricken to outrun the fire.

'How terrible to have lost such trees,' said Gerald. 'Why, where I live in the Highlands there's hardly a tree to be seen. We can blast off without the risk of a blaze like this – there's nothing to burn but the heather. Here, I imagine you've got to be awfully careful.'

'You have, Gerald,' said John.

He stopped and looked squarely at Lucky.

'All dragons have to be careful,' he said.

'Don't look at me!' said Lucky. 'I never . . .' and then she stopped and looked around and recognized the spot where she had blazed off at the rabbits.

'Oh no!' she said.

'Oh yes,' said John.

'It was me?'

'It was you.'

'Oh dear,' said Gerald.

'Oh John!' cried Lucky. 'You knew! And you didn't say anything in front of Mummy and Daddy.'

'I nearly didn't say anything in front of anyone ever again,' said John. 'Bart and I only just made it to the lake.'

Two huge tears rolled out of Lucky's eyes.

'What can I say?' she whispered.

Well, you could say you were sorry, thought John.
That's all I want you to say, I suppose.

'I'm . . . so . . . so . . . sorry,' said Lucky.

'That's all right,' said John. 'Don't cry.'

'No, don't cry, Lucky,' said Gerald.

'I can't stop!' sobbed Lucky. 'To think, I nearly
frizzled my own brother. And poor Bart too. How
could I be so careless and thoughtless and selfish and
stupid? I'll never breathe fire again, never!'

'Oh yes, you will,' said John. 'Just take a bit more
care, that's all.'

'I will! I will! Oh, John dear, you do still love
me?'

'Of course I do.'

So do I, thought Gerald. She looks so revolting
with the tears running down her face like that.

'Dry your eyes now,' said John. 'It's all over and

done with. Gerald, why don't you take Lucky off for a nice little flight? Get her to show you the rest of the forest, and maybe pick up a snack somewhere, eh?'

'Good idea,' said Gerald. 'Come on, Lucky, let's go.'

'Will you be all right by yourself, John?' sniffed Lucky.

'Of course I will,' said John, and he watched them take off in a swirling cloud of ash, and fly away.

He walked on, out of the burned area, into the greenwood. Odd, he thought, to be without Bart, Bart who was his eyes and ears and nose, his protector, his friend.

Thinking about his wolf, full grown now, and remembering that first sight of him as a tiny, starving, black cub, John wandered on, mile after mile, in a dream, all his woodcraft forgotten.

He was walking under a big sycamore tree when suddenly he heard the twang of a bowstring and the sudden hiss of an arrow that passed a yard above his head and stuck quivering in the trunk beside him.

Quick as a flash, John flung himself behind the sycamore. Tomfool, he said to himself angrily, to be taken by surprise in your own forest. Bart would have warned me long ago of this fellow, whoever he is. And I have no weapon of any sort.

He considered taking to his heels, but then decided against it. The man who had shot that arrow might

well be an expert bowman, aiming to miss. Next
time, it might be to hit. He waited. There was
nothing else to do.

After a while he heard a stick crack and then
almost immediately a voice, quite close.

'Put your hands upon your head,' said the voice,
'and stand out from behind the tree.'

John did as he was bid.

Facing him was a rough-looking, bearded man.
Another arrow was fitted to the string of his longbow and it pointed straight at John's thumping
heart.

'Od's bodkins!' said the man. ''Tis but a boy. I

had thought ye to be a King's man, one o' they damned verderers that do plague honest forest folk.'

Honest forest folk, thought John! I know who this fellow is for sure. He's an outlaw, one of many sought by the Sheriff for wrongdoing. They take refuge in the depths of the forest and prey upon travellers. He knew also that the verderers, forest officers responsible both for the trees and for the red deer, were

always on the look-out for these outlaws, who poached the royal game, the penalty for which was hanging.

'Please!' he said. 'I have done you no harm.'

'Nor will,' said the bearded man. 'For all I know ye're the son of a King's man, ready to run home and bring the lawmen after me. And I've no wish to swing from a tree.'

'No, no!' said John. 'I am an orphan. I have no father, nor mother.'

'A likely tale,' growled the outlaw. 'A big, strapping, well-fed lad like you, dressed in good clothing!' and before John could move, the man flung down his bow and grabbed him by the collar. He pushed his bearded face into John's and smiled. It was not a nice smile.

'Ye'll tell no tales, my lad,' he said. 'Will ye now?'

'Oh no,' said John. 'I won't say a word.'

'Ye won't,' said the outlaw.

From a sheath on his belt he drew a dagger.

'Because,' he said pleasantly, 'I'm going to cut your throat.'

Earlier Bart, who had been lying under the oak as he had been bidden, his great head on his paws, his brown eyes fixed on the spot where he had last seen his master, had suddenly risen to his feet.

This in itself was odd, for normally the black wolf, once given the order to sit or lie down, would have sat or lain for ever and a day.

Next, he began to whine, and, as Albertina came out to see what the matter was, Bart threw back his head and pointed his muzzle at the sky and howled. Then he was gone, running full tilt down the field.

Something of his anxiety communicated itself to the she-dragon, and, pausing only to blow a cloud of dust from the threshold of the cave, she flew after him.

By now the surface of the forest floor had cooled a good deal, and Bart was able to cross it without hurt, but on its charred surface the scent he was following, of John and the two young dragons, went dead.

From above, Albertina saw him casting eagerly about, a black shape on a black background, and then he reached the unburned side and with a yelp picked up the trail again.

On ran Bart, nose to ground, with the wolf's lope that eats up the miles, while Albertina flapped above, catching sight of him now and again between the trees. Then suddenly she saw his head come up as he approached a big sycamore, and his lope changed to a full gallop.

By the time Albertina landed, it was all over.

Even as the outlaw raised his dagger, he heard a sudden thud of feet and then, before he could turn, a heavy body struck him squarely between the shoulder-blades and knocked him flying.

'You should have seen it!' said Albertina to the other
dragons later. 'There's this fellow, flat on his back,
white as a sheet, with Bart lying on his chest. And
John kicks the dagger out of his hand and he says to
Bart "Get off," and to the man he says "Get up."
By that time, of course, I've arrived and when he
sees me, he goes as green as you, Lucky. There's
John patting Bart and stroking my face, the dear
boy, and I thought the chap's eyes would pop right
out of his head. And then John picks up the dagger
again. "No! No!" the fellow screams. "Spare me,
dragon boy, spare a poor man's life!" "Well, let's see
now," says John. "You'll not be needing your longbow, will you?" "No, no!" "Nor your arrows?"
"No," says the man and he picks up the bow and

the arrow that's fitted to it, and he unslings his quiverful, and he even pulls out another arrow that's stuck in the tree and hands the whole lot over. "You're fortunate," says John. "My friend here," and he points to me, "has given up eating people. That would have been a nasty death for you." Then he brandishes the dagger. "You won't be wanting this?" he says. "No, no." "Then it's my turn to use it." "Oh mercy!" yells the fellow and he puts both hands to his throat and John steps forward and the dagger flashes out.'

'He killed him?' said Montagu and Lucky and Gerald with one voice.

'He cut through the waistband of his breeches,' said Albertina, 'clean as a whistle, and they fell down round his ankles. "Go now!" says John, "and tell your friends — if you have any — not to tangle with the dragon boy." And off goes this outlaw chap, holding up his breeches with both hands, and glancing back over his shoulder like a hunted hare, tripping over brambles and falling into holes, till at last he disappears among the trees. Laugh? I thought I'd die!'

19

John Little

One morning some weeks later, at the start of winter, Gerald Fire-Drake and John were alone in the cave. Lucky had gone down to the picnic area to help her parents with some cooking, but although she had asked Gerald to come too, he had pleaded a headache.

'Sorry about your headache,' said John.

'I'm afraid that was a bit of a fib, John,' said Gerald. 'I wanted to get you on your own. I need your opinion.'

'Oh,' said John. 'What about?'

'Well, it's like this,' said Gerald. 'I think I should fly north.'

'To your home in Scotland, you mean?'

'Yes. I really think I ought to make it up with the Laird.'

'The Laird?'

'That's how my father is known. I feel awfully bad about falling out with him. My mother was very upset too.'

'Well, then I think you should go.'

'Yes. That wasn't what I was going to ask you about. Look, do you fancy a flip? We could fly off somewhere quiet.'

'Oh, that would be nice,' said John. 'I haven't flown for ages,' and after telling Bart to stay and guard the cave, he climbed up on to Gerald's beige back and wedged himself in one of the fin-saddles, and away they went.

Gerald landed again after a short, but, for his rider, a very pleasant flight, and John climbed down.

'Now, what's all the mystery?' he said.

'I'd better tell you straight, dragon to man,' said Gerald. 'I want to marry your sister.'

'Gadzooks!' cried John. 'That's marvellous!'

'I think she cares for me,' said Gerald.

'I'm sure she does.'

'But I don't want to go to Scotland with nothing arranged. I mean, I may be gone some time.'

'Ask her then.'

'Yes. But will her parents approve, do you think?'

'Ask them,' said John. 'No, better still, ask Montagu, formally, you know.'

'I'll have to get the Laird's permission too,' said Gerald. 'We're both under age, after all.'

'The sooner you get started, the better,' said John. 'Fly me back now and go and find Lucky and take her for a walk. And the best of British luck to you!'

*

So it was that that evening, while John and Montagu and Albertina were sitting chatting, Gerald appeared in the mouth of the cave, followed by Lucky. She looked very pleased with herself, John saw, indeed her green cheeks seemed slightly rosy, though that might have been a reflection from the firelight of the older dragons' breath.

Gerald approached Montagu.

'Sir,' he said, 'I have come to ask for your daughter's paw in marriage.'

'My dear boy!' spluttered Montagu. 'I . . . I don't know what to say!'

'Yes, you do, Monty,' said Albertina.

'Yes, you do, Daddy,' said Lucky.

'Yes, I do!' shouted Montagu. 'Of course, Gerald, of course, I give my consent most willingly. I am delighted, we are delighted, aren't we, Hotlips?'

'We are indeed, dear Gerald,' said Albertina. 'But do not forget that ours is not the only approval you must seek.'

'I know, Mrs Bunsen-Burner,' said Gerald. 'I thought to fly to Scotland tomorrow. I may have to be away some time, which is why Lucky and I want to be at least unofficially engaged.'

'You are!' shouted Montagu. 'You are, as from this moment. And if Hamish Fire-Drake is the dragon I take him for, he'll make no objection to an official engagement.'

'Though that may have to be quite a long one,'

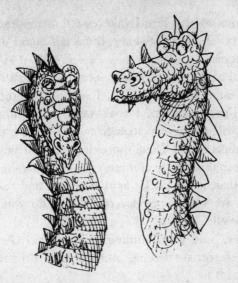

said Albertina. 'You are both very young.'

'I can wait, Mummy,' said Lucky. 'I can wait for ever!'

'Well, not for ever, I hope,' said Gerald. 'Perhaps a couple of years though.'

'And then we'll give you a slap-up wedding!' said Montagu. 'What a feast we'll have! Tell you what, Gerald, my boy, how would it be if we all flew up to see your people next spring? I'd like to chew the fat with old Hamish again, and then we could maybe fix a date.'

'Good idea, sir!' said Gerald. 'Then I can repay some of the hospitality that you and Mrs Bunsen-Burner have shown me,' and he gave Montagu directions to the Fire-Drake estate, a modest little property of about twenty thousand acres in the Highlands.

Amid all the excitement, John had sat silent, his arm around Bart. One day, I suppose, he thought, when I'm grown up, I shall want to get married. But it will seem very strange to live among people again. Sometimes I feel more dragon than boy, I'm so used to this family of mine.

'Brother,' said Lucky as though she had read his mind, 'are you happy for me? What do you think about it all?'

'Sister,' said John, smiling, 'I think that Gerald is a very fortunate fellow, and the best dragon you could wish for.'

'The best dragon certainly,' said Lucky, 'but when we are married, you will be the best man, won't he, Gerry?'

'None better,' said Gerald.

'Funny,' said Lucky next morning.

All the thank yous and good wishes and promises for the future and farewells had been said, and Gerald had flown away north.

'What's funny?' said John.

'To think that before so very long, I shall be Mrs Fire-Drake. It will be strange not to be a Bunsen-Burner any more. You're not one, of course, are you, because Mummy and Daddy adopted you? But you must have a surname, though I never thought to ask you before. What is it?'

'Little,' said John.

'John Little – that's your real name?'

'Yes.'

'How odd, when I've always thought of you as little John.'

(How could Lucky have guessed that in a dozen years' time little John would have grown into a giant of a man, the tallest and strongest in all Mercia.)

John laughed. 'I'm getting bigger,' he said. 'I'm ten now, but you can't expect me to grow as fast as you do, you know. We are quite different creatures after all.'

'I know,' said Lucky, 'and I shall never hold it against you that you have the misfortune to be so handsome, John, honestly I shan't.'

'Ah,' said John. 'We can't all be as ugly as you. You're the ugliest dragon ever.'

'That's what Gerry said,' sighed Lucky, staring dreamily northwards.

Gerald Fire-Drake was not the only thing to fly.

Time flew too.

Before you could look round, it seemed, winter had given place to spring, and the Bunsen-Burners had set out to visit the Fire-Drakes in the Highlands. Albertina had had some misgivings about leaving John on his own, but she need not have worried. Of all the boys in Merrie England, John was probably the best equipped to look after himself.

First, he was well armed. He was big enough and strong enough now to pull the longbow that he had taken from the outlaw, and he practised daily, shooting at a target such as a knot on a tree trunk until he became so skilled a bowman that he could have knocked a squirrel out of the top of the tallest tree. Not that he did, for though he recognized that meat-eaters, like himself and the dragons, must kill for food, the idea of killing for sport was repugnant to him.

As well as the bow, he had the dagger, and the old knight's sword, now of a size that he could handle. He had hit upon the idea of using Montagu as a mobile blacksmith's forge to heat the sword blade red-hot, so that he could shorten and sharpen it.

And then, of course, he had Bart. The black wolf was the perfect guard – strong, swift, intelligent and loyal, who would, he knew, fight to the death for him against any enemies, human or animal.

But then again all seemed to steer well clear of John. Maybe the outlaw had spread the word among his kind about the dragon boy, and maybe, somehow, the wild beasts knew of the deaths of the brown bear and the wolf-pack. Whatever the reason, John and Bart walked the forest unchallenged, happy in each other's company.

One fine evening they were playing in the field below the cave, John throwing a stick and Bart

racing after it and bringing it back, when the wolf
suddenly dropped the stick and raised his head,
staring at the northern horizon. John looked, but

though he could see nothing, he knew that Bart had somehow sensed the coming of the dragons, and sure enough, ten minutes or so later, they came in sight, beating steadily along in line abreast, Lucky between her parents.

Albertina and Montagu came gliding in to land, but Lucky flew high overhead and John saw her port wing drop and her starboard wing lift, as over she went in the victory roll.

The Laird, it would seem, had approved the match!

20

'What a Happy Time'

'The Laird, of course,' said Albertina, 'and Lady Flora.'

Another year and more had passed and the family were drawing up the guest list for the approaching wedding feast.

'And Gerry's brothers and sisters,' said Lucky. 'There are three each of them.'

'That's eight so far then,' said Albertina. 'John, you keep count, can you?'

'Then there's family,' said Montagu. 'My brother and his wife.'

'Ten,' said John.

'I didn't even know you had a brother, Daddy,' said Lucky.

'Haven't spoken to him for thirty years, but they'll have to come.'

'And my cousins, I suppose,' said Albertina.

'How many?' said John.

'Three.'

'That's thirteen then.'

'What cousins, Mummy?' said Lucky.

'Three of the prettiest, most empty-headed she-dragons you'll ever meet, darling,' said Albertina. 'Can't stand 'em, but there, blood is thicker than water.'

'We'd better invite the Examiner,' said Montagu. 'He did pass Lucky first time, and I don't expect the poor old chap often gets a square meal.'

'All right,' said Albertina.

'Fourteen,' said John.

'Who else?' said Albertina.

'Tell you what,' said Montagu. 'We'll ask the Charmouths. Nice sort of people, and with seven daughters to marry off, it should ensure us a few wedding invitations in the future. And you never know, Gerald's brothers might be interested.'

'Twenty-three,' said John.

'What about that Welsh trip you made, dear?' said Montagu. 'Anyone there you'd like to invite?'

'No,' said Albertina.

'That's it then, I should think. Add you and me, and, of course, the bride and groom.'

'And you have twenty-seven dragons,' said John. 'Quite a lot to cater for.'

'Zounds!' said Montagu. 'You're right there, John. We shall need a few tons of meat. What's it to be, Hotlips – a mixed grill?'

Albertina considered the matter.

'We're talking about August,' she said (the first day of that month was the appointed date). 'It may well be very hot. What do you think of the idea of a cold buffet, Lucky darling? With a good selection of different dishes, of course. That way we could have everything cooked and garnished – you'll help, John dear, won't you? – and laid out ready before anyone arrives. It will save all the hassle of a barbecue on the day, and, after all, if anyone wants hot food, they can easily heat it themselves.'

'That's fine by me, Mummy,' Lucky said. 'Where shall we have it though? We can't get all that lot in the cave.'

'Be a tight squeeze in the picnic area,' said Montagu.

'Why not have it beside the lake?' said John. 'It solves the problem of drinks, and the young ones would probably enjoy a bathe afterwards.'

'John!' said Albertina. 'Whatever should we do without you!'

They needed him too for his culinary skills as the day approached. The spit in the picnic area was in constant use. One or other dragon supplied the heat to cook the huge quantity of prey that was brought in, while John basted and flavoured every kind of joint of meat.

There was beef with wild horse-radish sauce, and pork with crab-apple sauce, and lamb with mint sauce, and venison with whortleberry jelly. And there was fish from the lake – poached pike and croquettes of carp and eels cooked in a jelly made from the feet of calves. There was even a pair of roasted swans as a centre-piece to this great display of food, beside which someone now slept on guard each night to protect it from the beasts of the forest.

On the evening of the last day of July, the Fire-Drakes arrived from Scotland, and while Gerald and Lucky wandered away to whisper sweet nothings to one another, and the six youngsters went off to the lake for a late swim, the adults sat down in the cave to a light supper of sucking-pig, while John and Bart guarded the feast.

'Not too tiring a journey, I trust, Lady Flora?' said Montagu.

'Oh, do please just call me Flora,' said Gerald's mother. 'No, no, we had a pleasant flight. There was a tail wind that helped greatly, didn't it, Hamish?'

'Indeed,' said the Laird. 'And very good it is to be here in such surroundings. Gerald told us how hideous your cave was, Monty and, er, Albertina, and my word, he's right.'

Albertina simpered.

'Of course we can't compare with you in size, Hamish,' said Montagu. 'Five or six thousand acres of forest, no more. But it's well stocked, though I say it myself.'

'This sucking-pig is excellent,' said Lady Flora.

'We don't get such delicacies,' said the Laird. 'Mountain goat, more likely, though, of course, we do have plenty of deer. But then, so do you, I dare say, Monty?'

'Wait till tomorrow, old boy,' said Montagu. 'You name it, we've got it.'

On the morrow the other guests began arriving.

The Examiner was first, for he had no distance at all to come, followed by Montagu's brother and sister-in-law from Northumbria, and Albertina's three female cousins who had flown up from London. Last of all came Mr and Mrs Charmouth from Wessex with their seven daughters, all of whom eyed Gerald's brothers with great interest.

'Nice to see you again,' said Montagu after he had introduced them. 'The hunting been good, this last season?'

'Oh yah!' said Mrs Charmouth. 'Had some absolutely rippin' days.'

'The sprogs have been going like good 'uns,' said Mr Charmouth. 'Yoicks! Tally-ho! What?'

Judging by the interest with which all the guests were eyeing the cold buffet, Montagu thought it best to start things moving straight away, so that the feast could then commence.

He had asked the Examiner, who was accustomed to being called upon for such formal proceedings, to conduct a short civil ceremony.

When everything was ready and a space cleared, Montagu walked into it, Lucky by his side, and handed her over to Gerald who stood waiting with John. Then the Examiner, who was positively dribbling with hunger, said hastily, 'Gerald – Lucky – I now pronounce you dragon and wife,' and everyone made a rush for the food.

John had had the forethought to set aside something for himself and for Bart, which was just as well or else they would surely have been squashed flat as twenty-seven dragons pushed and shoved and gorged themselves.

Compliments flew thick and fast.

'Deelishush!' said the Examiner with his mouth jammed full.

The Laird swallowed one of the roast swans at a gulp.

'First-class feast,' he said, turning to Mrs Charmouth. 'Don't you agree?'

'Oh yah!' said Mrs Charmouth. 'Simply smashin'!'

As for Albertina's three London cousins, who had made the journey out to the sticks expecting the plainest of country fare, they could hardly have been more pleasantly surprised, though, to show how cosmopolitan they were, they spoke in French. So that when Albertina in passing heard one of them say '*Haute cuisine!*', she thought it was probably a catty remark and disliked them the more.

The feeling of well-being induced in Lucky's uncle by such a meal led him to address his brother for the first time in thirty years.

'Not bad,' he said, but Montagu did not answer.

At last everyone stopped eating (they had to, for there was nothing left but bones) and Montagu went to find John.

'Time for your speech,' he said.

'Oh, must I?' said John.

'Of course. It's expected.'

'I shall never be heard, or seen, amongst that lot.'

'Yes, you will,' said Montagu.

'Do you remember, dear boy,' he said fondly, 'when you first learned to swim, how you used to use the top of my head as a diving-board? Well, use it again – as a pulpit.'

So once again John clambered up the warty flank of his friend, and climbed the long neck, and stood upon the flat platform of the great head. He had dressed in his best clothes, and his thinnest, for it was a very hot day, and now he pulled off his squirrel-skin hat and stood waiting nervously.

'Ladies and gentlemen!' shouted Montagu. 'Pray silence for the best man!'

A respectful hush fell upon the assembled guests, broken only by the sound of the boldest Charmouth girl, who had eaten much too much, being sick in the bushes.

Whatever shall I say, thought John, looking around from his high perch at all the watching dragon faces. Then he saw Lucky, standing with her Gerald, and suddenly it was all easy.

'Friends,' he said. 'Those of you who have not met me before may know by now that I am Lucky's adopted brother.'

He paused, thinking – do I reveal that it was I who in fact hatched her? No, no, that would put Albertina in a very bad light. So he went quickly on, 'And no one, I venture to say, could have such a jolly, good-hearted, high-spirited, affectionate and, of course, last but not least, such a hideously ugly sister.'

'Hear! Hear!' called the Laird loudly, and there

was a round of applause.

'She is Lucky,' said John, 'but, oh, how lucky I have been to belong to so fine a family as the Bunsen-Burners.'

'Rah! Rah!' cried Mrs Charmouth.

'And what a lucky dragon the bridegroom is!'

Everyone cheered again, except the Examiner, who, overcome by food, had fallen asleep.

'And now,' said John, 'I know that the happy couple are anxious to get away on honeymoon, so will you all please join me in wishing long life and all possible happiness to . . . Gerald and Lucky!'

'Gerald and Lucky!' shouted the wedding guests, and Montagu lowered John gently to the ground.

'Good boy,' he said. 'You did that beautifully.'

Soon all the goodbyes had been said, and the bride and groom flew away over the lake, wing-tip to wing-tip. They headed due east, for they were bound for that beach where first they had met and where Albertina and Montagu had honeymooned, long years ago.

John stood between the Bunsen-Burners, a hand on each great side, and they watched until the young lovers were lost to sight.

'Oh Monty!' sniffed Albertina. 'She looked *so* revolting!'

'Don't cry, Hotlips,' said Montagu. 'We've still got our John, just like old times.'

Later on that first August day, when all the wedding guests had flown away, and Albertina and Montagu had retired to the cave for a little snooze, and the first scavengers were slinking down to the lakeside to gnaw at the ruins of the feast, John and Bart sat under the oak tree.

'Five years,' said John, 'I've been a dragon boy, and what a lot has happened in that time, eh, Bart?'

The black wolf's bushy tail went to and fro, while he gazed at his master with adoring eyes.

'But what a happy time it's been,' said John.

He got to his feet, picking up a stick from beneath the oak.

'Fetch, Bart!' he cried, and he flung it far down the field.